THE PERSIAN GULF WAR

"The Mother of All Battles"

Zachary Kent

—American War Series—

Enslow Publishers, Inc.

40 Industrial Road
Box 398
Berkeley Heights, NJ 07922
USA

PO Box 38
Aldershot
Hants GU12 6BP
UK

http://www.enslow.com

> *"The mother of all battles has begun."*
>
> —Iraqi President Saddam Hussein on Baghdad radio, January 16, 1991.

Library of Congress Cataloging-in-Publication Data

Kent, Zachary.
The Persian Gulf War: "the mother of all battles" / Zachary Kent.
p. cm. — (American war series)
Includes bibliographical references and index.
ISBN 0-7660-1730-3 (pbk)
ISBN 0-89490-528-7 (library ed.)
1. Persian Gulf War, 1991—Juvenile literature. [1. Persian Gulf War, 1991.] I. Title. II. Series.
DS79.72.K39 1994
956.704'42—dc20 94-2533
CIP
AC

Printed in the United States of America

10 9 8

To Our Readers: All Internet addresses in this book were active and appropriate when we went to press. Any comments or suggestions can be sent by e-mail to Comments@enslow.com or to the address on the back cover.

Illustration Credits: AP/Wide World Photos, p. 17; Department of Defense, pp. 7, 9, 23, 25, 27, 31, 33, 35, 37, 39, 41, 43, 46, 48, 50, 57, 60, 62, 65, 67, 69, 77, 79, 83, 84, 86, 91, 93, 96, 99, 101, 103, 105, 109, 111, 113, 115, 116; Enslow Publishers, Inc., pp. 13, 81.

Cover Illustration: Department of Defense, Still Media Division.

Contents

Foreword. 4

1 Bombs Over Baghdad 5

2 Lines in the Sand 12

3 A Shield in the Desert 30

4 Operation Desert Storm 52

5 "The Mother of All Battles". 72

6 The 100-Hour War. 89

7 The Aftermath 108

Chronology. 119

Notes by Chapter 121

Further Reading and Internet Sites . . 125

Index 126

Foreword

During the summer and fall of 1990, thousands of American soldiers, sailors, and air force personnel performed duty in the Persian Gulf. As part of Operation Desert Shield they defended the eastern border of Saudi Arabia against a possible invasion by Iraq. Americans at home tried to boost the morale of these servicemen and women by sending letters of support. In September 1990, I sent one letter addressed to "Any Service Member."

"Dear Service Member," the letter began. After describing where I lived in New Jersey, I explained that my job was writing American history books for young people. Then I continued,

> I can just imagine how bored you must get sometimes out there in the Middle East. So I thought I'd send this letter to help break up your day.
>
> It's exciting and fun to write about American history. But I think what you're doing is far more important. You're actually out there making history. You have every right to be proud of the contribution you're making. Everyone I've heard or spoken to believes it's right that the United States should be in the Middle East right now. I hope the Kuwait crisis reaches a fast and peaceful solution and that you're able to return home real soon.
>
> The weather in New Jersey has been pretty hot lately. It has been getting up into the 90s the last few days. Still I guess that's about 10 degrees cooler than it is where you are. Professional football season is getting started. It's hard to guess which teams will do well this year. Being a New Jerseyan, of course, I'll be rooting for the Giants.
>
> Stay cool and keep your spirits up!
>
> Best wishes,
> Zachary Kent

After many tense months, on January 17, 1991, war erupted in the Persian Gulf. The Americans who charged into combat at that time certainly made history in proud and startling fashion.

"The liberation of Kuwait has begun."

—White House spokesman Marlin Fitzwater to reporters
January 16, 1991

1 Bombs Over Baghdad

Bright flashes and streaks of colored light suddenly filled the skies over Baghdad, Iraq. "An attack is under way," exclaimed ABC newsman Gary Shepard. He was reporting from the Iraqi capital early in the morning of January 17, 1991.

"There's a very big explosion!" declared Tom Aspell of NBC News who was also on the scene. "Red tracers, white tracers! It's going up all over the place!"

Across the United States, Americans crowded around their television sets for news. The United States, leading a United Nations (UN) coalition, had begun an air attack on Iraq. The coalition's mission was to end the Iraqi occupation of Kuwait. As the bombing continued, most television networks lost contact with Baghdad. Only the

Cable News Network (CNN), a 24-hour news channel, was able to keep its line open. In a room on the ninth floor of the Al Rashid Hotel in Baghdad, CNN reporters Bernard Shaw, Peter Arnett, and John Holliman provided a live account of the start of the Persian Gulf War from inside the enemy capital. No live, videotaped pictures could be transmitted, but viewers heard the reporters' voices. Throughout the world people listened to a war as it happened.

"Something is happening outside," Bernard Shaw first reported. The noise of Iraqi anti-aircraft fire echoed in the background. "Peter Arnett, join me here," Shaw called out. "Let's describe to our viewers what we're seeing . . . the skies over Baghdad have been illuminated . . . we're seeing bright flashes going off all over the sky . . . Peter."

"Well, there's anti-aircraft gunfire going into the sky . . . " declared Arnett. "However, we haven't heard the sound of bombs landing, but there's tremendous lightning in the sky, lightning-like effects . . . Bernie."

"I have a sense . . . " Shaw continued, "that people are shooting toward the sky and they are not aware or cannot see what they are shooting at. This is extraordinary. The lights are still on. All the streetlights in downtown Baghdad are still on. . . . We're getting starbursts in the black sky . . . Peter."

"Now the sirens are sounding for the first time . . ." explained Arnett. He handed the microphone to John Holliman, who just then arrived in the room. "Good evening, gentlemen . . . or rather good morning," Holliman calmly said. "I cannot see any aircraft in the sky here . . . a lot of tracer bullets going up in the sky, but so far no planes. . . ." The electricity suddenly went out, plunging the entire hotel into darkness. "Wow! Holy Cow!" Holliman cried, hitting the floor as a giant explosion shook the hotel. "That was a large airburst that we saw . . . it was just filling the sky."

"And I think, John, that burst took out the telecommunications," Peter interrupted. "You may hear the bombs now. If you're still with us, you can hear the bombs now. They're hitting the center of the city!"[1]

Television viewers listened as the three men described

A Tomahawk missile streaks skyward, launched from the U.S.S. *Wisconsin* at the start of the Persian Gulf War. On the first day of fighting, one hundred Tomahawks smashed targets in Iraq.

what was happening. The reporters scurried around the room on hands and knees, talking nervously amid the sounds of sirens and deafening explosions. Tracer fire, streaking missiles, and bursting bombs lit the Baghdad sky.

"The sky is lighting up to the south with anti-aircraft fire," Holliman explained. Then there was an explosion in the background and the reporters' voices exclaimed, "Oooooh," then "Oooow." "Bombs are now hitting the center of the city. War has begun in Baghdad."

After more than an hour, Holliman remarked that the first portion of the attack had ended. "It was like the fireworks finale on the Fourth of July at the base of the Washington Monument," he declared.

"There were four or five waves of bombing," Arnett summed up. "I think they were F-15Es. It has been deathly quiet for the last fifteen or twenty minutes."

"I'm lying on the floor," added Shaw. "The sky over Baghdad is black. It is eerily quiet. There is a cool breeze blowing through the window. It occurs to me that I didn't get dinner tonight."[2]

Arnett resumed. "This was a surprise attack."

"This is meant to be a sample," Shaw explained of the bombing. Then attacks in the distance seemed to flare up. Shaw declared that he saw "the sky light up, red, yellow, orange. It's possible that planes are pounding targets fifteen or twenty miles [twenty-four or thirty-two kilometers] from here."

"Every bomb seems to be hitting something," remarked Arnett.

"Peter, look at this . . ." exclaimed Holliman, "a bright flash of light that seems to be a—it seemed to come across from north to south, and even came up here by us in the hotel. And there it goes—almost like a shooting star."

"I think that shooting star is probably an F-15, John," commented Arnett.

"So that's what they look like at night when they're working," marveled Holliman. "All right. It's good to know. . . ."

"Yes, John," Arnett continued, "that was a heck of a strike. The plane could have been as close as 500 meters

An armed and dangerous American F-16C Fighting Falcon prepares to take off from Saudi Arabia in the first daylight attack against Iraq on January 17, 1991.

in the sky above its target. This certainly has been met with a lot of anti-aircraft fire, but it is long gone at this point, John."

"Yeah," added Holliman. "These planes are moving so rapidly, and with the one bright light on them. I guess that's the engines themselves that we're seeing going by. This is something that I've never covered before, ladies and gentlemen."[3]

Unable to sleep during the next hours, Shaw kept coming back to join Holliman on the air. "It was one hell of a night," Shaw later declared. "Wave after wave of planes. It shook you to your soul."

Around 10:00 A.M. the bombing started again, and Holliman was back on the air.

> There have just been two very loud explosions that rocked us here in downtown Baghdad. . . . I can't tell you exactly what just happened, but it shook us up a bit. . . . There's a rumbling coming from the west, like a herd of horses. I hear now what sounds like big bombs falling but I don't see anything. But I hear this rumbling. I'm going to stick this microphone out the window and see if you can hear it too. . . . There's a lot of thunder and it's obviously not coming from the heavens, but from the coalition forces.[4]

In Baghdad, Shaw, Arnett, and Holliman continued to report the sights and sounds of war. It was the first time ever that a war's opening engagement was broadcast live. Overseas, reporters and world leaders also watched the all-news channel for information about the crisis. CNN finally lost contact with its three Baghdad reporters after sixteen hours, when Iraqi military officials shut down the phone line. But the beginning of the Persian Gulf War's Operation Desert Storm was the most watched television event in history.

"In the life of a nation, we're called upon to define who we are and what we believe. Sometimes the choices are not easy."

—U.S. President George Bush, August 8, 1990

2 Lines in the Sand

One man alone was responsible for the Persian Gulf War—Saddam Hussein, president of Iraq. He ruled his nation with an iron fist, demanding the complete loyalty of his people. "Saddam, we will give our blood for you!" Iraqi children were taught to chant in the streets of Baghdad.

Rise of a Dictator

The Middle East nation of Iraq had been created from part of the defeated Turkish Ottoman Empire at the end of World War I. In a tent in the Arabian desert in November 1922, British high commissioner Sir Percy Cox had opened a map and chosen what became the Iraq-Kuwait border. The new border denied Iraq a good outlet to the Persian Gulf. Iraq's coastline on the gulf

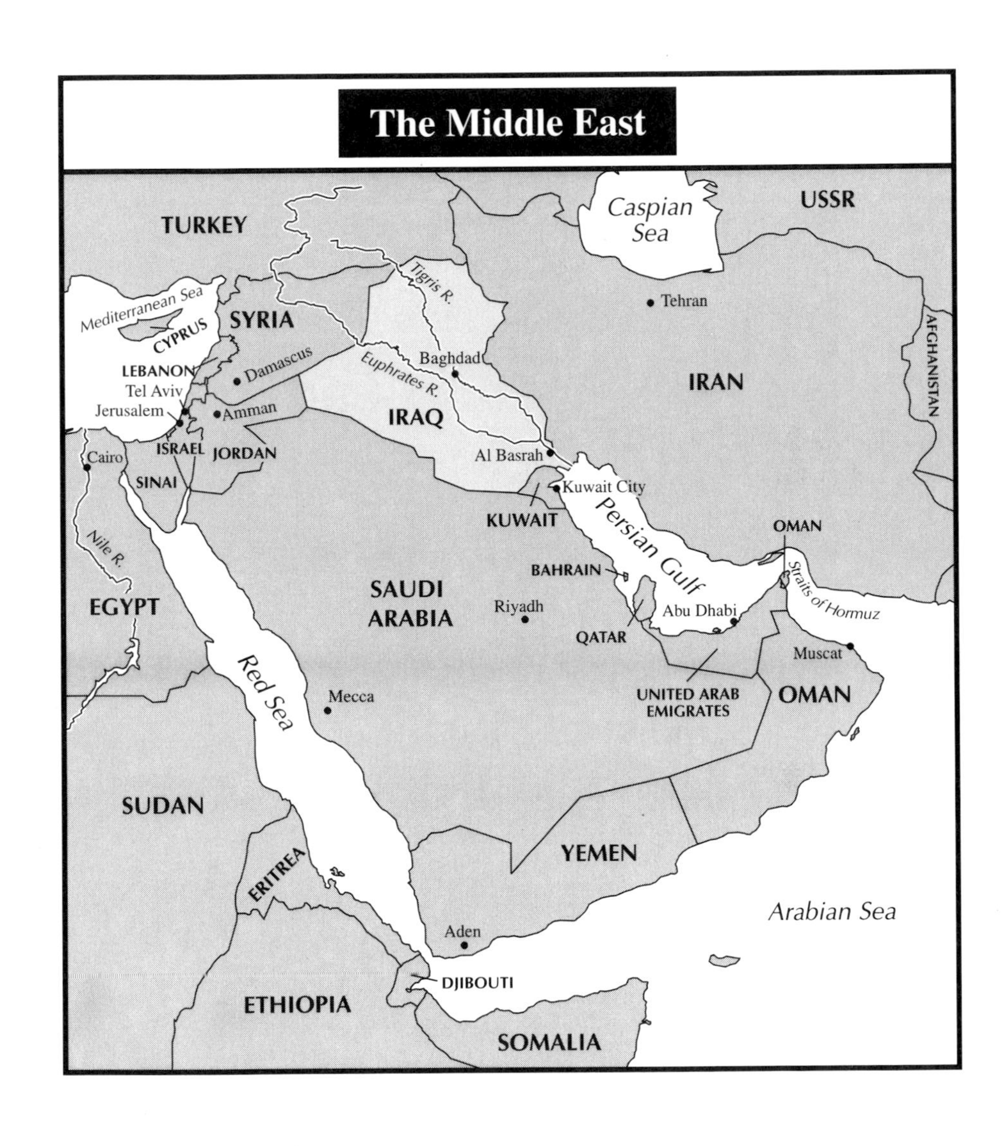
The Middle East
TURKEY
Caspian Sea
USSR
Mediterranean Sea
CYPRUS
SYRIA
Tigris R.
Tehran
AFGHANISTAN
LEBANON
Damascus
Baghdad
Euphrates R.
IRAN
Tel Aviv
Jerusalem
Amman
IRAQ
ISRAEL
JORDAN
Al Basrah
Cairo
SINAI
Kuwait City
KUWAIT
Persian Gulf
OMAN
Nile R.
BAHRAIN
Straits of Hormuz
SAUDI ARABIA
EGYPT
Riyadh
Abu Dhabi
QATAR
Muscat
Red Sea
UNITED ARAB EMIGRATES
OMAN
Mecca
SUDAN
YEMEN
ERITREA
Arabian Sea
Aden
DJIBOUTI
ETHIOPIA
SOMALIA

would be only 26 miles (42 kilometers) long. Sir Percy, wishing to finish his work, had made his decision quickly.

As a result, Saddam Hussein grew up in the new nation of Iraq. He was born on April 28, 1937, in a village of mud and reed huts near Takrit, beside the Tigris River. In 1957 twenty-year-old Saddam joined the small radical Iraqi Baath political party. In Arabic, the chief language of the Middle East, *Baath* means "renaissance" or "resurrection." The Baath Party hoped to bring back to life the great ancient Islamic empire of the region. The Baath Party attracted many thugs and murderers into its ranks, all of whom hoped to seize power by force. Saddam showed a special enthusiasm for weapons and violence.

In 1959, Saddam and other Baathist triggermen attempted to assassinate General Kassem, the military dictator of Iraq. Later in 1968 General Ahmed Hassan al-Bakr took power. He made thirty-one-year-old Saddam Hussein deputy secretary-general. Saddam's chief job was running Iraq's ruthless security police. When Al-Bakr resigned in July 1979, Saddam quickly seized control and made himself the new Iraqi president.

Past dictators, Adolf Hitler of Germany, and Joseph Stalin of the former Soviet Union, were two of Saddam Hussein's heroes. He also admired the character of Don Corleone, the mob leader in the movie *The Godfather*. In a bloody purge, Saddam swiftly executed hundreds of Iraqi politicians and military officers. As many as 500 of Saddam's suspected enemies were shot by firing squads during the new president's first few days in office.

Saddam used poison gas to crush a rebellion of Kurds in northern Iraq in 1979. Some 5,000 innocent Kurdish men, women, and children died in the village of Halabja. In September 1980, after months of skirmishing, Saddam Hussein invaded Iran, the nation to Iraq's east. Eight years of bloody battle followed. By July 1988, when Iran accepted a cease-fire, hundreds of thousands of Iraqis and Iranians had died in gruesome trench warfare. The war had cost Iraq $500 billion, leaving it $80 billion in debt.

During its war with Iran, Iraq had become the world's largest arms importer. By 1990 Iraq, with 1 million troops, possessed the world's fourth largest military force—after the Soviet Union, China, and the United States. Much of Iraq's military equipment was modern, and many of its army commanders and troops were combat veterans of the Iran-Iraq War.

Saddam Hussein soon developed a brutally simple strategy. He would use the power of his army to get his nation out of debt. At a 1990 conference of Arab nations, Saddam demanded help from his rich neighbors in the Persian Gulf. "I need $30 billion," he bluntly remarked, "and if they don't give it to me, I'm going to take it from them."

In a blistering speech on July 17, 1990, Saddam blamed sinking oil prices and the OPEC (Organization of Petroleum Exporting Countries) members for Iraq's problems. In early 1990, oil was selling for $20.50 a barrel. By summer, the price had dropped to $13.60. Iraq's oil wells provided much of that nation's income. Each dollar drop meant a $1 billion per year loss for Iraq, worsening Iraq's financial problems.

Now Saddam openly threatened to use force against any Arab oil-exporting nation that continued to pump too much oil. In particular he blamed the ruling Sabah family of Kuwait, Iraq's tiny neighbor to the south. Kuwait is a small, oil-rich nation with a population of just 2,090,000—compared with the 18,000,000 people of Iraq. Yet Kuwait possessed huge oil reserves and a valuable gulf coastline stretching 120 miles (193 kilometers).

Besides producing oil above the OPEC quotas, Saddam accused Kuwait of slant-drilling, or drilling under Iraq from Kuwait, into the Rumaila oil field. This oil lay beneath the ground of southern Iraq and northern Kuwait. He claimed that the Kuwaitis were stealing oil that rightfully belonged to Iraq. "The oil quota violators have stabbed Iraq with a poison dagger," Saddam angrily declared on July 17. "Iraqis will not forget the saying that cutting necks is better than cutting means of living. Oh, God Almighty, be witness that we have warned them!"[1]

Through the next days Saddam massed Iraqi troops along the Kuwaiti border. At 2:00 A.M. on August 2, 1990, Saddam Hussein's troops began to take Kuwait by force.

Invasion!

Loud explosions shook awake U.S. Army Major John F. Feeley, Jr., at dawn on August 2, 1990. He was staying in a room at the Kuwait International Hotel in Kuwait

Saddam Hussein, president of Iraq. To get his nation out of debt, the brutal dictator demanded money from his oil rich neighbors in the Persian Gulf. "If they don't give it to me, I'm going to take it from them," he bluntly warned.

City. "I looked out my window and saw flashes across the horizon," Feeley later recalled. "It was like lightning, except it was coming from the wrong direction. It was coming from the ground up."

In the morning darkness some 100,000 Iraqi troops began crossing the border into Kuwait. These troops included eight divisions of the Iraqi Republican Guards—the best soldiers in Saddam Hussein's army. Columns of Iraqi tanks roared along the six-lane superhighway toward Kuwait City, 80 miles (129 kilometers) south of the Iraq-Kuwait border. Iraqi jet fighters and armed helicopters soared over the advancing troops.

The invading Iraqi attack force outnumbered the entire Kuwaiti armed forces two to one. The surprised Kuwaitis were quickly overrun. The Iraqis smashed into Kuwait City as the morning sun rose into the sky. With no time to lose, the ruling emir of Kuwait, Sheik Jabir al-Ahmad al-Jabir as-Sabah, and other members of the Kuwaiti royal family escaped in limousines. They headed south to Saudi Arabia. Some pilots of the Kuwaiti air force also retreated into Saudi Arabia, to fight another day.

In the Kuwaiti capital, Iraqi tanks surrounded the central bank, where Kuwait's gold reserves were stored. Tanks also surrounded the Ministry of Information building, which housed Kuwait's radio and television studios. Shortly after 6:30 A.M., the fight concentrated around the emir's grand Dasman Palace. A few gallant Kuwaitis defended the palace. Sheik Fahd, the emir's brother, waited at the top of the palace steps as the first

Iraqis arrived. He stood in their way with a drawn pistol. An Iraqi officer casually shot him dead.

Some Kuwaiti military units resisted before being mowed down by the ruthless firepower of the Iraqi soldiers. The noise of machine guns, rifles, and Iraqi anti-tank weapons filled the streets of Kuwait City. In the center of the city's business district armored personnel carriers, filled with Iraqi troops, crunched through the streets. Soviet-built T-72 tanks flanked the armored vehicles. In seven hours the invasion was all over.

On August 8, over Baghdad radio, Saddam Hussein announced the permanent annexation of Kuwait as Iraq's nineteenth province. "We are now one people, one state that will be the pride of the Arabs," he predicted. Meanwhile the ruin of Kuwait had begun. Torture, killings, and mass arrests started on the day of the invasion. Kuwaiti men and women were randomly pulled off the streets for questioning by Iraqis.

During the next days more than 1.5 million people fled Iraq, Kuwait, and other gulf countries close to the fighting. They included more than 700,000 Egyptians, 400,000 Kuwaitis, 250,000 Palestinians, and more than 350,000 Asian workers—most of whom were from India, Pakistan, Bangladesh, Sri Lanka, and the Philippines. More than 750,000 refugees escaped into Jordan. Within weeks the International Red Cross and other organizations supplied food, blankets, tents, and other relief to these displaced persons.

Many refugees from Kuwait told frightening stories of torture and execution by the Iraqi invaders. Weeping mothers and fathers described sons taken from them at the border, and friends and loved ones left behind. "They took my best friend Bedar, and the next day they dropped his body in the street," a Kuwaiti doctor grieved. "They had wrapped his head in a Kuwaiti flag and fired three bullets into his skull."[2]

During the early days of the occupation, twenty-one Kuwaiti university professors refused to take down a picture of the emir and replace it with one of Saddam. They were all said to have been executed. In addition Iraqi looters stripped everything of value from Kuwait. They completely emptied stores, and even shipped animals from the Kuwaiti National Zoo north to Iraq.

Some Kuwaitis formed an anti-Iraq guerrilla movement. Using guns, grenades, explosives, and even shoulder-fired missiles, the guerrillas launched attacks. In mid-August they fired a rifle grenade at the Iraqi Embassy. Kuwaiti guerrillas also claimed they shot down several Iraqi helicopters. These Kuwaiti efforts for freedom only made the Iraqi invaders more violent.

The conquest of Kuwait had been swift and complete. But Iraq looked as if it were not planning to stop there. Iraqi Republican Guard divisions next massed their tanks and artillery along the border of Saudi Arabia, moving supplies forward with them. Iraqi troops might cross into Saudi Arabia at any time.

This Will Not Stand

On the White House lawn, U.S. President George Bush responded to the Iraqi invasion of Kuwait on August 6,

1990. "I view very seriously our determination to reverse . . . this aggression," he declared. "This will not stand. This will not stand! This aggression against Kuwait."

Later, Bush admitted, ". . . I worried that Saddam's intentions went far beyond taking over Kuwait. With an attack on Saudi Arabia, he would have gained control over a tremendous amount of the world's oil supply."

Immediately following the invasion, the UN Security Council passed Resolution 660, calling for Iraq's immediate and unconditional withdrawal from Kuwait. UN Resolution 661 was also drafted. It ordered the halt of international trade with Iraq. However, the effect of such an embargo would take time. And the embargo would not stop Saddam's tanks from dashing south into Saudi Arabia.

Moving swiftly, Bush sent U.S. Secretary of Defense Dick Cheney and General H. Norman Schwarzkopf to Saudi Arabia. They arrived on August 6 to confer with Saudi King Fahd Ibn Abdel-Aziz about the threat of an Iraqi assault on Saudi Arabia. "We don't know what he is going to do," Schwarzkopf explained to King Fahd. But Saddam could have his tanks deep inside Saudi oil fields, the general said, "easily within forty-eight hours."[3]

"We want you to come," King Fahd immediately responded, inviting American troops into his country. The Arab world might condemn his decision. The Islamic nations of the Persian Gulf regarded Westerners with suspicion. But Saudi Arabia needed help fast. The next day, August 7, President Bush ordered United States military aircraft and soldiers to Saudi Arabia. Some United

States warships were already in the Arabian Sea and the Persian Gulf, with more on the way. The massive buildup was given the code name "Operation Desert Shield."

"As today's President, I ask for your support in the decision I've made to stand up for what's right and condemn what's wrong all in the cause of peace," Bush announced in a speech from the White House Oval Office on August 8, 1990. He continued:

> At my direction, elements of the 82nd Airborne Division as well as key units of the U.S. Air Force are arriving today to take up defensive positions in Saudi Arabia. . . . Let me tell you why. . . . With more than 100,000 troops along with tanks, artillery and surface-to-surface missiles, Iraq now occupies Kuwait. . . . There is no justification whatsoever for this outrageous and brutal act of aggression. . . . Four simple principles guide our policy. First, we seek the immediate, unconditional, and complete withdrawal of all Iraqi forces from Kuwait. Second, Kuwait's legitimate government must be restored. . . . Third, my administration . . . is committed to the security and stability of the Persian Gulf. And fourth, I am determined to protect the lives of American citizens abroad. . . . America does not seek conflict. . . . But America will stand by her friends.[4]

On August 16, Saddam ordered all American citizens in Kuwait to report to three big hotels in downtown Kuwait City. By August 22, several thousand Americans, Britons, French, and other Westerners had been moved from the hotels to Iraqi defense locations in Kuwait to serve as "human shields." "You are going to receive some American bodies in bags," the Iraqi leader warned Bush.

Millions of Americans were outraged by such threats. In a speech on August 20, President Bush declared, "We have been reluctant to use the word 'hostage.' But when Saddam Hussein offers to trade the freedom of those citizens of [the] many nations he holds against their will in return for concessions, there can be little doubt that . . . they are, in fact, hostages."

The situation in Kuwait worsened as the disciplined Republican Guards were withdrawn and units of poorly trained Iraqi volunteers replaced them. Iraqi soldiers

United States troops arrive in Saudi Arabia aboard a giant C-5A Galaxy aircraft at the start of Operation Desert Shield. On August 8, 1990 President Bush announced he was sending American forces to "assist the Saudi Arabian government in the defense of its homeland."

seeking food randomly entered houses. They stole stereos and television sets, jewelry, and other personal possessions. Kuwaitis who offended Iraqi soldiers were shot in the streets.

In Saudi Arabia, Operation Desert Shield began to take shape. The United States had drawn a line in the sand. Soon President Bush could tell the U.S. Congress, "Iraq will not be permitted to annex Kuwait. And that's not a threat, not a boast. It's just the way it's going to be."

The Generals

". . . we see in Saddam Hussein an aggressive dictator threatening his neighbors," declared President Bush. To protect Saudi Arabia, Bush would rely on two American generals—General Colin L. Powell and General H. Norman Schwarzkopf.

Powell served as the Chairman of the Joint Chiefs of Staff. "Nobody could provide you with better guidance . . ." former Secretary of Defense Frank Carlucci once said of Powell. "He is extraordinarily bright, articulate, and with excellent judgment."

Powell was born in the Harlem section of New York City in 1937. His parents had emigrated from Jamaica many years before. They taught their son the importance of study and hard work. ". . . there was simply an expectation that existed in the family—you were supposed to do better," remembered Powell.[5] Powell attended the City College of New York. By the time he graduated at the top of his Reserve Officer Training Corps (ROTC) class in 1958, he knew a career in the Army was for him.

General Colin L. Powell, Chairman of the Joint Chiefs of Staff. As President Bush's top military advisor, Powell provided the vital command link between the White House and United States military headquarters in Saudi Arabia.

Powell served in the Vietnam War in 1962 and 1963. One day in the Vietnam jungle he stepped into a Punji-stick trap. The sharpened stick impaled his left foot, causing an ugly wound. Powell returned for a second tour of duty in Vietnam in 1968. During the 1970s and 1980s he continued to rise through the military ranks. In 1987, he received promotion to the important post of National Security Advisor. He reported directly to President Ronald Reagan.

Two years later, President Bush chose Powell to become the Chairman of the Joint Chiefs of Staff. Bush stated that he "will bring leadership, insight, and wisdom to our efforts to keep our military strong and ready. . . . It is most important that the chairman . . . be a person of breadth, judgment, experience, and total integrity. Colin Powell has all those qualities and more."

In his new post Powell ran the Pentagon, distributing the $290 billion a year military budget. He also acted as the chief military advisor to the President. In 1989, he helped plan Operation Just Cause, the invasion of Panama in Central America that overthrew the country's corrupt leader—General Manuel Noriega. At the White House in the summer and fall of 1990, Powell briefed President Bush and Secretary of Defense Cheney at least once a week. He described the numbers of tanks, troops, aircraft, and ships as they arrived in the Persian Gulf.

General Schwarzkopf was assigned command of Operation Desert Shield. He would be in charge of all the troops in the Persian Gulf. Born in 1934, Schwarzkopf spent his early years living in Morrisville, New Jersey.

General H. Norman Schwarzkopf, Commander-in-Chief of the U.S. Central Command. The tough soldier in charge of Operation Desert Shield was called “Stormin’ Norman” by his troops.

Schwarzkopf's father was superintendent of the New Jersey State Police and a West Point graduate. It seemed natural that young Norman would attend West Point too. One of Norman's West Point teachers later remembered, "I was immediately struck by his leadership ability and quick alert mind. . . ." In 1956 Schwarzkopf graduated from West Point, number 43 in a class of 480.

As an advisor with the Vietnamese Airborne Division and then as commander of an American Army battalion, Schwarzkopf survived combat in the Vietnam War in 1965–1966 and 1969–1970. When he pulled a wounded soldier out of a mine field, he won his third Silver Star for bravery. Like Powell, Schwarzkopf rose through the military ranks. His soldiers nicknamed him "Stormin' Norman."

In 1988, Schwarzkopf was named Commander-in-Chief of the U.S. Central Command. At Central Command his job was to plan for possible United States military operations in nineteen Middle East countries, including Saudi Arabia. "He's a good guy to go to war with," described retired Admiral Joseph Metcalf, "because he's a good solid commander. He's a soldier; he's more comfortable out with the troops than he is in the Pentagon."

On August 27, 1990, General Schwarzkopf arrived in the Saudi Arabian capital city of Riyadh. Inside a bunker beneath the Saudi Ministry of Defense building he set up his Desert Shield headquarters. Together, generals Schwarzkopf and Powell would plan to confront Saddam Hussein.

"Someone once asked me what is the difference between me and Saddam Hussein," Schwarzkopf later declared. "The answer is I have a conscience and he doesn't. . . . In my mind he is an evil man."[6]

General Powell also frankly stated his belief:

> Saddam Hussein says it's between the haves and have-nots. He's right. He has Kuwait, he stole it, and the world community rightfully insists that he give it back. That's what this conflict is all about, pure and simple: between what is moral and what is immoral, between what is right and what is wrong.

"If the Iraqis are dumb enough to attack, they are going to pay a terrible price."

—U.S. General H. Norman Schwarzkopf,
August 27, 1990

A Shield in the Desert

American troops moved into the Persian Gulf region with amazing speed. They did not know how long they would need to be there. But they were prepared to stay and do their duty.

Building a Coalition

The first United States unit to reach Saudi Arabia was the ready brigade of the 82nd Airborne Division, which was swiftly dispatched from Fort Bragg, North Carolina. The troops began to arrive on August 9, 1990. Teams of operations people, air-traffic controllers, loadmasters, logistics managers, communications specialists, and intelligence officers also flew into Dhahran, Saudi Arabia, on C-141 StarLifter cargo planes. Soon 747s, DC-8s,

DC-10s, and other aircraft were airlifting troops and material to the Persian Gulf.

The aircraft carrier U.S.S. *Independence*, which had been in the eastern Indian Ocean, neared the Persian Gulf on August 7. That same day the U.S.S. *Eisenhower* passed through the Suez Canal. Meanwhile, another carrier, the U.S.S. *Saratoga*, and the battleship U.S.S. *Wisconsin* departed the United States from east coast ports enroute to the Middle East. On August 8, the first F-15

On the way to the Persian Gulf, the U.S.S. *Dwight D. Eisenhower* passes through Egypt's Suez Canal. The mighty nuclear-powered aircraft carrier was among the first United States warships to take part in Operation Desert Shield. In time, United States naval forces in the Gulf region would include six aircraft carriers and two battleships.

Eagle fighters joined the carriers in Saudi Arabia, having flown nonstop from Langley Air Force Base in Virginia. At the end of the first week, ten squadrons of F-15 and F-16 fighter planes had reached Saudi Arabia.

General Schwarzkopf worried that the Iraqis might charge into Saudi Arabia before it was fully defended. He was relieved when the 7th Marine Expeditionary Brigade from California arrived in the gulf on August 15. On August 26 the 1st Marine Expeditionary Brigade from Hawaii arrived. The Army's 24th Infantry Division (Mechanical)—based at Fort Stewart, Georgia—traveled 8,000 miles from Savannah to the port of Dhahran aboard fast cargo ships. On August 27, the ships began unloading that division's M1A1 tanks and Bradley fighting vehicles. By the start of September, more than 40,000 United States soldiers were in the Saudi Arabian desert. The rest of the force for Desert Shield was on its way.

"You could have walked across the Mediterranean on the wings of the C-5s, C-141s, and commercial aircraft," recalled civilian pilot Mike Carlozzi. By early September 375 military cargo and transport aircraft, joined by many commercial aircraft, had flown more than 2,000 missions to the gulf, delivering 106 million pounds of cargo. Officers involved in the massive airlift called it "the aluminum bridge to the Middle East."

Merchant, or cargo, ships arrived in Saudi Arabia, loaded with tanks, weapons, food rations, and fuel. By September 28, the Desert Shield sealift reached its peak with ninety ships at sea. "It was the quickest and largest military sealift buildup since World War II," General

Schwarzkopf later declared, "an 8,000-mile [12,882-kilometer], 250-ship haze-gray bridge, one ship every 50 miles [81 kilometers] from the shores of the United States to the shores of Saudi Arabia. And they offloaded some 9 million tons of equipment and petroleum products for our forces."[1]

Major General William G. "Gus" Pagonis had the task of organizing United States military transportation and supplies in Saudi Arabia. American soldiers deployed in Desert Shield arrived with only their weapons and a

A 5-ton truck with trailer drives out the front end of a giant American C-5B Galaxy cargo plane during Operation Desert Shield. In less than a month, United States aircraft delivered 106 million pounds of cargo to Saudi Arabia.

few personal belongings. Everything else—from ammunition to shoelaces—came through Gus Pagonis and his staff. Within 90 days, Pagonis and his men moved 1.3 million tons of equipment, including 12,000 tanks and 67,000 wheeled vehicles. In the coming months, Pagonis and his men would serve more than 88 million meals, deliver more than 152 million gallons of water, pump more than 94 million gallons of fuel, and distribute more than 236,300 tons of ammunition!

By early November 1990, the United States had assembled a military force of some 230,000 men and women in the gulf. On November 8, President Bush announced that America would commit up to 200,000 additional troops to the Persian Gulf, eventually raising United States troop levels to 430,000. Many of these troops were reservists, militarily trained civilians called upon to serve in this time of need.

The United States was not the only country outraged by Iraq's invasion of Kuwait. Thirty other nations were also sending troops, aircraft, and ships to the gulf, making up a truly international coalition. Egypt was the first country to send troops to join United States and Saudi forces. Troops from other far-flung countries included 170 Czechoslovakian chemical-warfare specialists and 2,000 soldiers from Bangladesh. France sent 15,000 troops, led by Lieutenant General Michel Roquejeoffre, including the famed Foreign Legion. Great Britain added 25,000 soldiers commanded by British Lieutenant General Sir Peter de la Billiere. These troops included the 7th Armoured Brigade, which traced its history to

A Syrian soldier stands at attention. Fifteen-thousand Syrian troops joined the coalition forces defending Saudi Arabia. Altogether, thirty-one nations sent troops, aircraft, and ships to take part in Operation Desert Shield.

the "Desert Rats" that had fought in North Africa in World War II.

Saudi Lieutenant General Khalid bin-Sultan received command of the Joint Arab Task Force that included Syrian, Moroccan, Kuwaiti, Omani, and other troops. U.S. Lieutenant General Charles Horner commanded some 1,800 United States warplanes and 435 Saudi, Kuwaiti, British, Italian, and French planes. Lieutenant General Walter E. Boomer would lead the U.S. Marines. Lieutenant General John J. Yeosock commanded the more than 280,000 U.S. Army troops. By January 1991 more than 500,000 coalition troops and airforce personnel were positioned in Saudi Arabia and on ships offshore.

By that time, 120 U.S. Navy ships were in the Persian Gulf, Arabian Sea, Red Sea, and eastern Mediterranean. Vice Admiral Stanley Arthur was the overall naval commander. The United States naval force included six aircraft carriers and the World War II battleships U.S.S. *Wisconsin* and U.S.S. *Missouri.* With nine 16-inch guns, both battleships could send 2,000-pound high-explosive shells against targets 20 miles (32 kilometers) away. "There's a lot of years left in these old gals," explained Captain David Bill, commanding officer of the *Wisconsin.*[2]

The American warships were joined by destroyers and frigates from Australia, Britain, Canada, France, Italy, and the Netherlands as well as smaller warships from the gulf nations. Together, they stopped and searched merchant ships in the gulf that could be steaming to or from the Iraqi port of Basra.

"More than 200 ships from 13 nations conducted over 10,000 flawless intercepts, which formed a steel wall around the waters leading to Iraq," recalled General Schwarzkopf. "Thanks to these superb efforts not one cargo hold, not one crate . . . of seaborne contraband ever touched Saddam Hussein's shores." The naval blockade caused Iraq to lose an estimated $30 million every day.

President Bush could be proud of the coalition build up in the Persian Gulf. The United States had led the way. In his State of the Union Address on January 29,

An Iraqi merchant ship intercepted in the Persian Gulf. A sailor on the U.S.S. *Goldsborough* points a .50 caliber machine gun, while a boarding team prepares to climb aboard the Iraqi vessel to conduct a search. The coalition's naval blockade prevented cargo from reaching or leaving Iraq.

1991, he proclaimed, "We are the only nation on this earth that could assemble the forces of peace."

The Clash of Cultures

"We'd only been here a month or two when we started to learn the rules of the country," remembered Lieutenant John Butler of the Army's 595th Medical Company.

The people of Saudi Arabia follow a culture very different from that of most Americans. The Islamic religion rules the lives of all Saudis. Saudi King Fahd is known as the "Keeper of the Faith." His country contains two of Islam's most holy shrines—at Mecca and at Medina. In Saudi Arabia all activity stops five times a day for prayer. The national constitution is the religious book called the Koran. Inviting foreign troops, most of them Christians as well as women and Jews, into the Muslim holy land was frowned upon by some in the Islamic world. The Americans had to adjust to the unfamiliar Islamic culture and various regional customs.

Just after arriving at Khobar, Saudi Arabia, some American troops heard a loud wailing that they believed was an air raid siren. Instantly they grabbed their gas masks and raced for the nearest bomb shelter. Soon, though, they realized the sound was a Muslim call to prayers—broadcast from the speakers of a neighborhood mosque.

Some American behavior annoyed the Saudis. They watched uncomfortably as United States soldiers shopped in local *souks*, or markets, with rifles slung on their shoulders. They also noticed female military personnel driving trucks in a society that forbids, by law, women to drive. The Saudis grumbled when soldiers set up camps in empty areas of desert that were, in fact, owned by Saudi citizens.

Thus, on August 30, 1990, General Schwarzkopf issued General Order No. 1 for Operation Desert Shield. The order pointed out that "Islamic law and Arabic customs prohibit or restrict certain activities which are generally permissible in Western societies."[3] Therefore, Schwarzkopf banned sexy magazines, including swimsuit and body-building publications. American women were

Dressed in traditional clothes, an Arab walks toward a camouflaged United States military radar station. Operation Desert Shield required both Americans and Arabs to make living adjustments.

instructed to dress modestly at all times. Female soldiers were told they could not bare their arms or legs in public. Shorts were prohibited, as were short sleeves and certain bright colors.

Saudi women are so concealed by their long black robes, or *abayas*, that American soldiers soon began referring to them as "BMOs" (black moving objects). Touching between men and women in public seldom occurs. Many Saudi women not only cover their head and face, but also wear gloves to insure that they do not touch men. There is no dating or dancing in Saudi Arabia. In addition there are no movie theaters, and alcoholic beverages are not permitted.

In Schwarzkopf's command of 430,000 United States troops, as many as 32,000 troops were women. American women served as pilots, mechanics, armed guards, military police officers, and in many other military positions. At one supply battalion, American women usually drove trucks, operated radios, stood guard duty, and ferried water and gas tankers. Once they left their base, however, these women soldiers had to behave differently. "We can't drive and we have to wear long sleeves and pants or a long dress to cover our legs," complained one female American officer.

The Saudis told the women in a Massachusetts reserve military police battalion that they could appear in Saudi towns out of uniform only if they wore long black dresses. They also had to walk twelve paces behind any man they accompanied, according to Saudi custom.

Sergeant Sherry L. Callahan described what she and

Air Force sergeant Angela Finn operates a forklift in Saudi Arabia. Thirty-two thousand American women served in the Persian Gulf. Working hard, they earned the respect of their fellow troops.

other American women felt after arriving in Saudi Arabia. "At first we were angry," said Sergeant Callahan, the assistant crew chief tending an F-15 fighter of the First Tactical Fighter Wing. "We were deployed here to save these people, and they don't want us because we're women." Saudi soldiers stared in shock when she worked elbow to elbow with men on the mechanics of her jet fighter. "At first they just didn't know what to say to me," she recalled. "But sometimes now they even ask me to help on their aircraft if they're behind."

Humvees and MRES

"We're going to stay out here and live out here," vowed Colonel Walt Mather of the U.S. 24th Infantry Division.

The average American soldier, airman, and Marine in Desert Shield was twenty-seven years old. In Saudi Arabia he wore a desert warfare uniform. The troops called the uniforms "chocolate chips," because of their mixed tan and brown design. The typical Marine, when prepared for action, carried an M-16 rifle. He wore a Kevlar helmet and a Kevlar flak vest—both bullet resistant. On his back were about sixty pounds (twenty-seven kilograms) of additional packed equipment, including bedroll, entrenching tool, and canteens.

As the chance of ground combat became more likely, so did the chances for chemical warfare. American intelligence believed the Iraqis were trying to build deadly nuclear missiles as well as biological and chemical weapons. People knew Saddam Hussein had used poisonous gas against the Kurds, his own people. So United States

Two American soldiers practice surviving in the Saudi Arabian heat while wearing protective suits and gas masks during a desert training drill.

troops drilled for hours each day wearing chemical-proof heavy equipment, including gas masks and protective suits. During daytime training exercises, combat units struggled up and down sand dunes in temperatures of 49° C (120° F). By 9:00 A.M. the sand was already so hot that it seemed to burn through the thick rubber soles of boots.

The troops preferred nighttime training, which was more practical. It kept down cases of sunstroke and heat exhaustion. In the dark, M1A1 Abrams tanks and Bradley fighting vehicles rumbled through the sand dunes. Often the tanks, freshly offloaded, were still painted forest green. In no time they were sent through the "tanning salon"—the soldiers' term for a coat of sand-colored paint that camouflaged the tanks. Against the miles and miles of real sand the newly painted tanks would be difficult to sight by Iraqi gunners. The United States military also sent thousands of sturdy cars and trucks to the Persian Gulf. Their official initials "HMMWV" stood for "high-mobility, multi-purpose wheeled vehicles." But the troops called them "hum-vees."

For food, the troops stationed in the desert most often dined on MREs (Meals-Ready-to-Eat). Packed in plastic pouches, the MREs offered such entrees as "Ham Slices in Natural Juices," "Meatballs in Spicy Tomato Sauce," and "Chicken à la King." With each main course the troops got a side order such as "Potatoes au Gratin." Also included were a variety of snack items such as cocoa, Kool-Aid, coffee, pound cake, chewing gum,

M&Ms, and oatmeal cookies. The troops often added the cocoa to their coffee—creating "Coco-Joe" or "Moco," a tasty hot drink. Army Warrant Officer Wesley Wolf, food service advisor during Desert Shield, came up with the idea of mobile food stands to serve hamburgers, hot dogs, and french fries beside the Saudi highways. The troops who eagerly ate there soon called them "Wolfmobiles."

Many troops found the desert overwhelming. Home for many soldiers was a lonely patch of camouflage netting stretched overhead. Morning showers consisted of a bucket of chlorinated water. It seemed as though snakes, bugs, spiders, and scorpions were the desert's only wildlife. Sometimes a wandering camel, a swaying palm tree, or a herd of goats added to the scenery. The sun scorched the soldiers during the day, but in the cool of the night the stars came out. "You should see the night," Army Specialist Larry Campbell wrote home to his wife. "The sky comes alive with a billion stars and a moon that seems as bright as a spotlight. It's like you can see the whole galaxy."[4]

Sometimes violent sandstorms, called *shamals*, blew through the camps. Every year dozens of these fierce "Big Winds" rip across the Arabian Peninsula. Such desert sandstorms kicked up sand and also blew down tents and other items. Army doctor Howard Heidenberg of the 595th Medical Clearing Company recalled the collapse of a friend's tent: "I reached for the corner of the tent . . . when, just like in the *Wizard of Oz*, the whole tent suddenly lifted up off of the ground and started to blow away."

Mostly, though, the troops remembered the sand. Returning from a flight, Air Force pilot Gary Porterfield wrote home, "It's nothing but sand. One big beach. I can't believe people actually live here." The sand was as fine as talcum powder. The powder found its way into weapons, engines, and the computers that direct modern warfare.

"It's a nuisance we can do without," Sergeant First Class Surender Kotnakota complained. "It requires a lot

United States troops play football in the desert in front of their "Humvee."

of extra effort to keep things clean." Air filters on trucks had to be changed every other day, rather than every 30,000 miles. M-16 rifles needed to be stripped and cleaned daily because their ammunition magazines kept clogging with the sand.

Specialist Darin Fitzgerald of the 24th Infantry Division declared, "Sometimes it's real bad. You pick sand out from between your teeth. You never get rid of it." But he added, "We do what we gotta do. Waiting and not knowing—that's the tough part."

Yellow Ribbons

". . . I know what it's like to be away from home for a long period of time," General Powell told troops while visiting an air base in western Saudi Arabia, "and I know the sacrifice that you're making and the sacrifices that your families are making. If it's a source of comfort to you, you need to know, really know, that the American people are solidly behind you."

In the United States, some protesters believed United States forces were in the Persian Gulf only to protect America's access to oil. They paraded with signs declaring "No Blood for Oil!" and "My Brother's Blood is Thicker Than Oil." Other Americans, however, insisted that Saddam Hussein's madness for power had to be stopped. Whatever the reasons for going to the Persian Gulf, almost all Americans supported the troops. One way United States citizens showed their support was by tying symbolic yellow ribbons around tree trunks and branches in their yards. During the fall and winter of

1990, millions of yellow ribbons decorated the American landscape.

For many of the troops the worst part of Desert Shield was the waiting. But as Army Warrant Officer Jerry Orsbern remarked, ". . . those care packages from home. The people back home really helped us survive by sending those packages."[5]

The average amount of mail received by each of the United States troops in the Persian Gulf was an astonishing 3.75 pieces per day! The people of Virginia Beach, Virginia, for example, sent gifts through the mail.

A grinning sailor stands among heaps of mail aboard the aircraft carrier U.S.S. *Kennedy* during Operation Desert Shield. Americans did not forget the troops in the Persian Gulf. "I got mail from people I hadn't heard from in years," remembered one grateful Marine officer.

The gifts included six tons of M&Ms and Turkish Taffy as well as 20,000 paperback books. ". . . all my guys have been flooded with letters and care packages. I've never seen so much stuff," declared Air Force Master Sergeant John Massengill.

Crates of oranges and boxes of cookies all came through the mail. "What I am delivering here is more important than gold," remarked Air Force Major Wally Vaughn, who helped letters and packages reach the troops in Saudi Arabia.

Letters sent "To Any Serviceman" were full of heartfelt encouragement for the troops. People of all ages sent their best wishes and their prayers. American schoolchildren wrote tons of "To Any Serviceman" mail. "I wish I could help," wrote Salome Welliver, a fourth-grader from Kansas City. "But I'm just a nine-year-old. I pray for you and peace. If a war starts, you can win. God bless you."

Some of the troops wrote back. Lieutenant Colonel David Wood of the 101st Airborne Division wrote a letter to a class of fifth graders. "The desert is huge," he told them. "The country is about one half the size of America and it's all desert. In every direction, there's only sand and hills."

Some American entertainers such as comedians Bob Hope, Steve Martin, and Jay Leno and sports star O.J. Simpson traveled to the gulf to spend time with the troops. President Bush also visited Saudi Arabia. On Thanksgiving, November 22, 1990, Bush spoke to U.S. Marines and British troops at an outpost in northeastern Saudi Arabia. He told them:

> . . . on this day, with all that America has to be thankful for, it is fair for Americans to say, 'Why are we here?' It's not all that complicated. There are three key reasons why we're here with our UN allies making a stand in defense of freedom. We're here to protect freedom, we're here to protect our future, and we're here to protect innocent life. . . . a bully unchecked today is a bully unleashed for tomorrow. . . . No American will be kept in the gulf a single day longer than necessary. But we won't pull punches. We are not here on some exercise. . . . we're not walking

President George Bush visits U.S. Marines in Saudi Arabia on Thanksgiving, November 22, 1990. "We're here to protect freedom," he told them. Seated to the president's right, First Lady Barbara Bush listens.

> away until our mission is done, until the invader is out of Kuwait. And that may well be where you'll come in.[6]

The long days of waiting in the desert passed, one after another. Soon the December holidays arrived. "At least we'll be having a white Christmas," joked Marine Lance Corporal Christopher Williams, using his imagination to transform the pale brown sand.

On Christmas Day 1990, General Powell visited soldiers in Riyadh, Saudi Arabia. The Chairman of the Joint Chiefs of Staff shook hands with GIs and joined in the work of filling sandbags. General Schwarzkopf also visited his men when he could. "I visited Marines dug in near the Saudi-Kuwaiti border," he later recalled. "Their attitude was: 'We're not going to war, sir, we're going home—and the direction of home happens to be through Kuwait.' "

"We knew we would win, but we had no idea what our casualties would be, how the American public would react, or even whether the coalition would hold together."

—U.S. General H. Norman Schwarzkopf

4 Operation Desert Storm

On November 29, 1990, the UN Security Council adopted Resolution 678. The resolution established a six-week deadline for Saddam Hussein to withdraw from Kuwait. The council authorized the coalition "to use all necessary means to . . . restore international peace and security in the area." Saddam was given until midnight, Eastern Standard Time, January 15, 1991, to decide.

Deadline

President Bush made repeated efforts to reach a peaceful conclusion to the standoff in the desert. He promised "to go the extra mile for peace." But he later revealed, "I became convinced early on that, if diplomacy failed, we would indeed have to use force." In a speech from the

White House, Bush warned, "If one American soldier has to go into battle, that soldier will have enough force behind him to win. . . ."

On December 6, Saddam asked Iraq's parliament to release the last of the foreigners he held in Iraq and Kuwait. Within two days about 565 hostages, including 175 Americans, returned home in time for the year-end holidays.

On January 9, 1991, U.S. Secretary of State James Baker met in Geneva with Iraqi Foreign Minister Tariq Aziz. Baker tried to hand Aziz a personal letter from President Bush addressed to Saddam Hussein. But after reading it, Aziz refused to accept the letter. The letter stated:

> Mr. President:
> We stand today at the brink of war between Iraq and the world. This is a war that began with your invasion of Kuwait; this is a war that can be ended only by Iraq's full and unconditional compliance with UN Security Council Resolution 678. . . . There can be no reward for aggression. . . . unless you withdraw from Kuwait completely and without condition, you will lose more than Kuwait. What is at issue here is not the future of Kuwait—it will be free, its government will be restored—but rather the future of Iraq. This choice is yours to make. . . . I hope you weigh your choice carefully and choose wisely, for much will depend on it.

As time passed, President Bush requested the support of the U.S. Congress in case war became necessary. During the debate in the House of Representatives, Majority Leader Richard Gephardt of Missouri told his peers: "In this vote, we are not Democrats. We are not Republicans. We are Americans. We expect and want the members to vote their conscience, what in their mind is the right thing for this country to do."

In the Senate, Senator Edward Kennedy of Massachusetts stood among those against the war. "Let there be no mistake about the cost of war," he declared. "We have arrayed an impressive international coalition against Iraq, but when the bullets start flying, 90 percent of the casualties will be Americans. . . . we're talking about the likelihood of at least 3,000 American casualties a week, with 700 dead, for as long as the war goes on."

After three days of debates, the House and Senate finally voted late in the afternoon of January 12. The resolution passed 52 to 47 in the Senate, and 250 to 183 in the House. Congress would allow the President to use force, if required, to end the gulf crisis.

Saddam mistook the open debate and differences of opinion in America as a sign of weakness. "Kuwait belongs to Iraq, and we will never give it up even if we have to fight over it for 1,000 years," Saddam exclaimed.[1] "Yours is a society which cannot accept 10,000 dead in one battle," he taunted. The Iraqi dictator had rapidly built up his force in Kuwait from 100,000 on August 2 to over 430,000 by the end of December. Thousands of Iraqi infantrymen dug trenches, erected barricades, and buried explosive mines. Altogether, about 545,000 Iraqi troops entered the war zone and prepared for a long siege.

"The number of Americans killed will exceed tens of thousands if a ground battle occurs with Iraqi forces . . ." boasted Baghdad Radio. "[The Iraqi troops] are trained in defensive combat to an extent that no other force in the world has reached."

Thunder and Lightning

Saddam Hussein failed to meet his deadline. The moment for action had arrived.

"Colonel, are you going to guarantee me 100 percent success on this mission?" General Schwarzkopf asked. Colonel George Gray, leader of a commando unit called the First Special Operation Wing, took a deep breath and answered, "Yes, sir." "Well," ordered General Schwarzkopf, "then you can start the war."

On the night of January 16, 1991, at a secret staging area 700 miles (1,127 kilometers) west of Dhahran, eight Apache AH-64 helicopters and four MH-53J Pave Low helicopters lifted off and headed north into Iraq. Flying without lights, at high speed, and just thirty feet (nine meters) above the ground, the helicopters had a vital mission: to destroy two Iraqi early-warning radar stations.

The helicopters zigzagged around the camps of Arab goat herders to avoid being heard. They ducked into ravines to fly under radar screens and weaved through a maze of Iraqi observation posts. As they reached one of the two targets, an Iraqi sentry spotted the helicopters and turned to run toward the bunker. The sentry never made it. A laser-guided Hellfire missile from an Apache ripped the compound just as he opened the door. Clusters of Hydra rockets and streams of 30-mm cannonfire smashed into the buildings. One of the United States pilots yelled into his radio, "This one's for you, Saddam."

Within four minutes both radar stations lay in burning ashes. The destruction of the radar sites opened an overhead pathway through which coalition aircraft could fly undetected into Iraq. That night the entire allied air force streamed in through the route opened by Colonel Gray's commandos.

At a Saudi Arabian air base, American Stealth pilots strapped themselves into their cockpits. One after another the aircraft roared down the runway into the blackness and headed north, toward Iraq. The unusual angular shape and construction of the Stealth jets made them practically invisible to radar detection. Each plane carried a single 2,000-pound laser-guided "smart" bomb. The F-117A Stealth attack fighters were the newest and most secret aircraft in the U.S. Air Force.

At 2:51 A.M., Baghdad time, on January 17, the first Stealth pilot pressed a button on his control stick and his laser-guided bomb smashed into an early warning radar control center about 160 miles (258 kilometers) southwest of Baghdad. Other Stealth fighters bombed the Iraqi Tower for Wire and Wireless Communications, the International Telephone and Telegraph building in downtown Baghdad, the Presidential Palace, radar centers, the Iraqi Ministry of Defense, the Air Force Headquarters, and an air-field in western Iraq. In less than fifteen minutes the pilots completed their bombing runs and headed back to base. Each of the pilots had delivered his bombs precisely onto his targets. Operation Desert Storm had begun.

At 3:05 A.M., the first of the U.S. Navy's Tomahawk cruise missiles also smashed into its target in the Iraqi capital. Minutes later another Tomahawk missile struck a communications building in Baghdad. Altogether 100 Tomahawks were launched on the first day of Desert Storm. They were fired from vessels in both the Red Sea and the Persian Gulf. Each Tomahawk carried a single 1,000-pound high-explosive warhead or smaller multiple

An F-117A Stealth fighter rises into the sky. The unusual design of these aircraft made them practically invisible to enemy radar. As Operation Desert Storm began on January 17, 1991, Stealth jets helped lead the attack on Iraq.

warheads. Vice Admiral Stanley R. Arthur called the Tomahawks the "reach out and touch someone" weapon.

In a letter to his American forces, General Schwarzkopf exclaimed, "Soldiers, sailors, airmen, and Marines of United States Central Command: . . . You have trained hard for this battle and you are ready. . . . My confidence in you is total. Our cause is just! Now you must be the thunder and lightning of Desert Storm. May God be with you, your loved ones at home, and our country."

In Washington, D.C., President Bush appeared on television and told Americans, "The U.S. goal is not the conquest of Iraq; it is the liberation of Kuwait." The coalition forces would, however, do whatever was necessary to prevent Saddam from being a future threat to world peace. Bush continued, "We are determined to knock out Saddam Hussein's nuclear bomb potential. We will also destroy his chemical weapons facilities. Much of Saddam's artillery and tanks will be destroyed. Our operations are designed to protect the lives of all the coalition forces by targeting Saddam's vast military arsenal."[2]

In the first three hours of Desert Storm, more than 400 combat planes, and 160 tankers and command aircraft swarmed across the dark skies of the Persian Gulf. Wave after wave of jets took off from Saudi air bases. More jets roared off the decks of U.S. carriers in the Persian Gulf and the Red Sea. In Baghdad, air-raid sirens wailed and anti-aircraft batteries sent a blizzard of tracer bullets and surface-to-air missiles into the air. Flashes of flak (anti-aircraft shells) burst high in the sky—orange, white, and yellow. From their cockpits, pilots saw the flak bursting around them in every direction.

Flying north toward Kuwait, pilots of an EF-111 Aardvark squadron saw the night sky lighting up about 50 miles (81 kilometers) ahead. "It was like camera flash bulbs goin' off as you approached," Lieutenant "Hack" Peahrson recalled. "They were bombs exploding on the horizon."

EF-111 pilot Lieutenant Colonel Damaso Garcia later exclaimed, "I remember thinking, 'Hell! They're trying to kill us!'" The anti-aircraft fire lit up his jet's cockpit as if it were broad daylight.

Throughout the day of January 17, 1991, American, Saudi, British, French, Italian, and Kuwaiti aircraft conducted additional attacks throughout southern Iraq and occupied Kuwait. Flocks of American F-15Es struck at fixed Scud missile launchers in western Iraq as well as Iraqi air-fields. British Tornados executed very hazardous low-level strikes against Iraqi air bases to blast craters in their runways.

Meanwhile American F-4G Wild Weasels, EA-6B Navy Prowlers, and F/A-18 attack jets were firing high-speed HARM missiles with 145-pound warheads at radar facilities. With pinpoint accuracy, one bomb dropped down the rooftop airshaft of Iraqi air force headquarters. Bombed bridges across the Tigris and Euphrates rivers sank in smashed ruins. B-52 bombers, based on the island of Diego Garcia in the Indian

An F-14A Tomcat fighter flies over the desert after successfully completing a mission during Operation Desert Storm. This jet belonged to Fighter Squadron 33 based on the aircraft carrier U.S.S. *America.*

Ocean, dropped cluster bombs on airfields in the southern part of Iraq.

"By early afternoon I was able to tell Powell in Washington that we'd completed fully 850 missions," recalled General Schwarzkopf. "We'd clobbered many of the 240 targets on our list."[3] Saddam's lakeside palace in Baghdad lay in ruins. The ITT communications building downtown was wrecked. Two important Scud missile sites in western Iraq were severely battered, and several suspected biological and nuclear weapons bunkers were blown up. At the same time, squadrons of sturdy U.S. A-10 attack jets were swooping down and firing on Iraqi frontline supply dumps.

High above Saudi Arabia large KC-135 aerial tankers flew in circles as they pumped thousands of gallons of jet fuel through refueling hoses and into combat aircraft. E-3 AWACS (Airborne Warning and Control System) aircraft, each with a large rotating radar dome mounted atop its fuselage, flew closer to the Saudi-Iraq border. Their radars swept the skies over southern Iraq, tracking aircraft movements. U.S. Navy weapon specialists huddled over computer consoles on their ships. They monitored Tomahawk missiles on their way to their targets.

By January 20, coalition pilots had flown more than 4,000 separate missions. They had knocked out many targets, including Baghdad's electricity and water facilities as well as missile sites, communication centers, military supply depots, and artillery sites. At a news conference on January 23, General Powell revealed the

An American KC-135 Stratotanker pumps fuel into an F-16C Fighting Falcon in midair during Operation Desert Storm. Refueling operations such as this allowed coalition jets to fly farther distances into Iraqi territory.

coalition's future plans for Saddam's troops in Kuwait: "Our strategy to go after this army is very, very simple. First we're going to cut it off. And then we're going to kill it."

Saddam's War Against the World

"Whoever collides with Iraq will find columns of dead bodies, which may have a beginning but not an end," Saddam Hussein had threatened. When war broke out, Saddam quickly showed his brutal methods of retaliation.

At 3:03 A.M., January 18, the Iraqi dictator fulfilled one of his ugly promises. The first of eight Iraqi Scud missiles landed in Israel. Six fell in and around the city of Tel Aviv, and two landed in Haifa. Though no one was killed in the attacks, 47 people suffered injuries and 1,587 apartments were damaged. Of all the weapons in Saddam Hussein's arsenal, the Scud would prove to be his best. The crude Soviet-built 37-foot-long (11-meter-long) missiles were simply aimed and launched into the air toward their targets. "The Scud was a clumsy, obsolete Soviet missile . . ." General Schwarzkopf later explained, "a weapon that could fly 300 miles [483 kilometers] and miss the target by a couple of miles with a warhead of only 160 pounds [73 kilograms]. . . . However, the Scud was effective as a terror weapon against civilian populations."

Carried on trailer-like mobile launchers, the Scuds were easily hidden in buildings or ravines by day, then moved into firing position at night. During Scud attacks, frightened Israelis donned gas masks and hurried into the sealed rooms that every household was urged to prepare. "We have our classes in sealed rooms and have to carry our gas masks around with us at all times," explained one eighth-grade Israeli student.[4]

By attacking Israel, Saddam hoped to provoke Israel into striking back. Then he could claim that the war pitted the Islamic Arab nations against their hated Jewish neighbor Israel and its American ally. He hoped to drive many of the Arab nations out of the UN coalition.

To protect against Scud missiles sent into Saudi Arabia, U.S. Patriot missile batteries had been installed in the busy port areas of Dhahran, al-Jubail, and Ad-Damman. On January 18, the Israeli government also accepted the protection of Patriot missiles. Patriot air-defense missile batteries manned by United States soldiers were transported from United States bases in Germany. There was no mistaking the Patriots as they streaked upward and smashed into approaching Scuds.

Fear of the Scuds always remained, however. "Putting on those charcoal-lined chemical suits with the first Scud alerts, you'd see your whole life pass before you," remarked Major Charlie Wright of the 92nd Medical Battalion in Saudi Arabia.

General Schwarzkopf remembered one Scud raid on Riyadh: "Sirens sounded throughout the city and Patriot batteries went on full alert; in our basement war room we made sure our gas masks were handy."

Saddam would fire a total of eighty-six Scuds—forty at Israel and forty-six at Saudi Arabia. Many were blown

A United States Patriot missile launcher awaits action in the Saudi Arabian desert. Patriot missiles proved to be a valuable defense against Iraqi Scuds.

up by Patriots. In Israel, one person was killed and 239 wounded. An estimated 9,000 apartments and homes were damaged in and around Tel Aviv. By January 20, U.S. Air Force Lieutenant General Charles Horner ordered between 600 and 700 combat aircraft into western and southern Iraq every twenty-four hours. Their only mission was to hunt and destroy Scud missile launchers.

In addition to Scud attacks, Saddam Hussein used another brutal tactic during the air war. He ordered his army to flood the Persian Gulf with slick, black, crude oil. The Iraqis dumped millions of barrels of oil into the Persian Gulf. The oil spread in a huge slick fifty miles (eighty-one kilometers) long and twelve miles (nineteen kilometers) wide, killing birds, fish, and other marine animals. The oil slick seemed designed to prevent expected landings by U.S. Marines on the beaches of Kuwait City. If the oil reached Saudi seaside desalination plants along the coast, it could cut off much of that country's supply of drinking water. President Bush quickly condemned the oil spill as "environmental terrorism."

The oil slick lay as thick as mud on the surface of the water. It involved twenty-five times the amount of oil leaked by the Exxon *Valdez* in Prince William Sound, Alaska, in 1989. The toxic oil endangered mangrove swamps, and beds of sea grass and algae. As the oil sank to the bottom of the gulf, it killed coral reefs and other marine life. Sharks, porpoises, dolphins, sea turtles, and sea walruses were threatened by the spill. Comorants, gulls, terns, flamingos, and other birds became covered with oil and could not fly. Hundreds of dead birds washed up on the shores of Saudi Arabia.

An estimated 294 million gallons (1.1 billion liters) of crude oil escaped from Kuwait's Sea Island supertanker terminal before raiding American F-111 jets bombed terminal pumps, reducing the oil flow to a trickle.

A Time for Heroes

The air war against Iraq saw many acts of heroism. U.S. Air Force Captain Steve Tate of the 71st Tactical Fighter Squadron scored the first aerial kill of Desert Storm the

Saddam Hussein flooded the Persian Gulf with crude oil from the pumps at Kuwait's Sea Island supertanker terminal. Raiding American F-111 jets soon bombed the pumps, cutting off the flow.

first night of the war. On an escort mission over Baghdad, Tate's radar picked up an enemy aircraft sixteen miles (twenty-six kilometers) away. Tate fired a Sparrow missile at the "bandit." "There was a large bright flash under my right wing, as the Sparrow dropped off and its motor ignited . . ." he later recalled. "It seemed to start slow and then pick up speed really fast. You could see the missile going toward the airplane, and about two seconds after the [missile] motor burned out, the airplane blew up. A huge engulfing fire billowed up. It lit up the sky. You could see pieces of the aircraft in the glare."[5]

On January 24, Saudi Arabian Captain Ayedh al-Shamrani, flying an F-15 fighter, shot down two Iraqi Mirage F-1s. "I just rolled in behind them and shot them down," he declared afterward. During the air campaign, coalition aircraft destroyed forty Iraqi aircraft in air-to-air combat. Most Iraqi pilots chose to flee to neutral Iran rather than fight. By February 4 nearly 150 Iraqi planes had flown to Iran. "They never launched. They ran before us . . ." commented one American flyer.

Altogether forty-one coalition planes—thirty-two from the United States and nine from other countries—were shot down by Iraqi ground fire. Some pilots and air crewmen died as a result. Other survivors were picked up, sometimes far behind Iraqi lines, by United States search-and-rescue helicopters. Several coalition flyers were captured by Iraqi troops. In violation of the Geneva Convention, which governs the treatment of war prisoners, the captured soldiers were displayed on television, forced to make statements, and told they would be used as human shields at Iraqi military sites.

U.S. Navy Lieutenant Jeffrey Zaun was a bombardier-navigator in an A-6E Intruder off the carrier U.S.S. *Saratoga.* Zaun and his pilot Lieutenant Robert Wetzel parachuted safely to the ground after ejecting from their damaged plane. But Wetzel was injured, and Zaun stayed with him instead of trying to escape. The Iraqis forced Zaun to make a videotaped statement. "I think our leaders and our people have wrongly attacked the

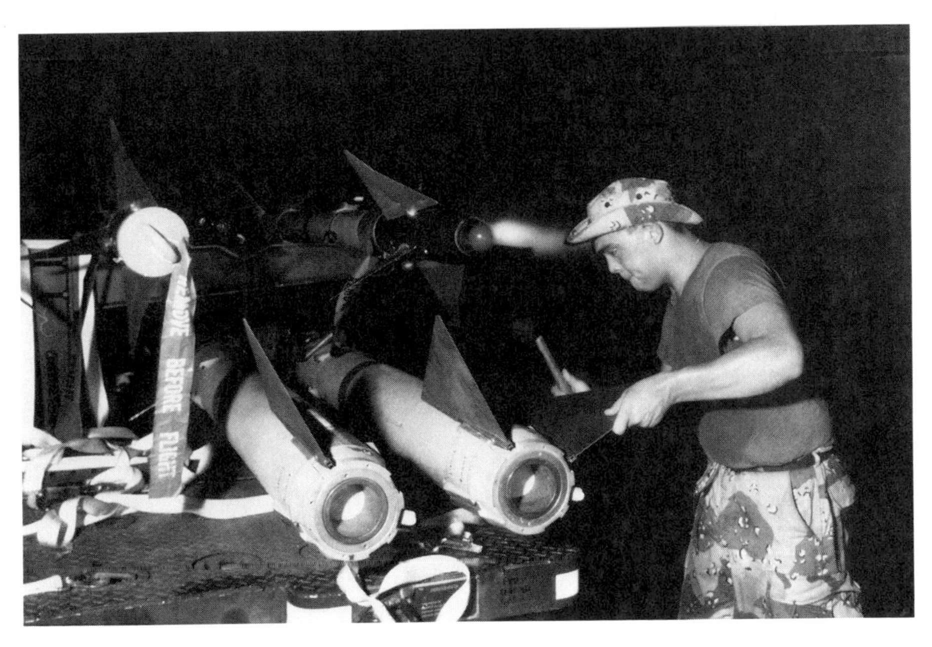

A U.S. Air Force specialist attaches a fin to a Sparrow missile during Operation Desert Storm. When ready, it will be loaded under the wing of a jet fighter. Ground crew often waited anxiously until their planes and pilots returned safely from a mission.

peaceful people of Iraq," Zaun slowly and unwillingly said.

Other captured coalition crewmen were forced to make similar remarks. "I think this war is crazy and should never have happened," stated Marine Chief Warrant Officer Guy Hunter, Jr., his blackened left eye nearly closed. This clumsy Iraqi propaganda only made Saddam Hussein more hated by the allies.

President Bush immediately condemned the Iraqi mistreatment of these prisoners of war. He said of Saddam Hussein, "If he thought this brutal treatment of pilots is a way to muster world support, he is dead wrong. . . ."

By mid-February 1991, coalition forces completely controlled the air over the Persian Gulf. General Powell announced on February 8, 1991: "Now the focus of the battle will shift to the Iraqi army in Kuwait, which is what we came here to do—kick them out. We tried to give [them] some good advice a few months ago. We told [them], 'Move it or lose it.' They wouldn't move it; now they're going to lose it." Iraqi tanks, artillery, short-range missiles, and troops increasingly became coalition targets.

Navy Commander Bud Bishop recalled, "The bombing was going on in Kuwait and Iraq around the clock. Probably every ten minutes there was someone going in or coming out. We would anchor off the coast, waiting for our target time, and we'd see a highway in the sky—a nonstop flow of aircraft."[6]

Coalition pilots bombed more than thirty bridges,

severing supply lines into Kuwait. "We get many many reports out of Kuwait that Iraqi soldiers are begging for food from Kuwait civilians," General Schwarzkopf reported.

On February 14, the Central Command claimed 1,300 Iraqi tanks were destroyed—30 percent of those in the Kuwait theater of operations. By February 24, intelligence officers guessed the number at 1,685—an increase of 385 in just ten days! U.S. Hercules cargo planes dropped 15,000-pound (6,803-kilogram) "daisy-cutter" bombs off of their rear loading ramps to smash Iraqi positions. The wear and tear on the soldiers' nerves, together with the lack of food and water, wore down the resistance of many Iraqi troops. No army in history had ever been subjected to such a relentless around-the-clock pounding. The Iraqi frontline forces seemed to totter near collapse. Day after day weary officers and enlisted men snuck through the lines to surrender in increasing numbers.

During the Persian Gulf War the coalition air forces dropped a staggering total of 141,921 tons of bombs on Iraq and Kuwait. "When we go north," declared U. S. Marine Lieutenant David Kirby, "I hope the Air Force has worked them over so well I can just push their soldiers over with my hands."

"The great duel, the mother of all battles, has begun."

—Saddam Hussein in a speech to Iraqi troops

5 "The Mother of All Battles"

The air war continued day after day. As the coalition troops on the ground tensely waited, they guessed it was only a matter of time before they would also get into the fight.

Khafji

Ground fighting in the Persian Gulf War began on January 29, 1991. That night forty-five tanks of the Iraqi 5th Mechanized Division drove 10 miles (16 kilometers) south across the Saudi border. The troops captured Khafji, an oil-processing town on the Saudi coast.

Twelve days earlier, Khafji had been deserted by residents fleeing out of the range of Iraqi artillery. There were, however, small advance units of Saudi soldiers and U.S. Marines in the town doing scouting and artillery spotting. "Khafji surprised us," admitted Marine Colonel Ron Richard afterward. "For the Iraqis it was a major spoiling attack."

As the Iraqi tanks advanced into the deserted town, the tank turrets were pointed backward, a universal sign of surrender. But then the turrets suddenly swung around, and the tanks started firing. "You couldn't tell which way they were coming from," a U.S. Marine sergeant later exclaimed. "It seemed like they were everywhere." Baghdad radio called the Iraqi attack "a sign of the thunderous storm that would blow across the Arabian desert and destroy America."

The few Marines in Khafji managed to hide from the invaders, some even hiding in a building occupied by Iraqis. The Iraqis controlled Khafji for about thirty-six hours. On Thursday, January 31, a counterattack forced them to retreat. Saudi and Qatari troops charged into the town, supported by U.S. Marine artillery, Marine Cobra helicopters, and F/A 18 and A-10 jets. In the action about twenty Iraqi T-62 tanks were destroyed and more than 400 prisoners were taken. The victorious Saudis marched through the streets of Khafji shouting and waving their national flag. It was the first land battle the Saudis had fought in the modern history of their kingdom.

New York Times correspondent Chris Hedges entered the town soon afterward. He reported:

> Numerous Iraqi, Saudi and Qatari armored vehicles, some with smoke pouring from the turrets, lay abandoned in the streets, several still

> holding the charred bodies of soldiers. Buildings and walls were pockmarked with bullet holes and, in many places, shattered by heavy shells. . . . The exhausted Saudi troops, their eyes red after two days of fighting, turned to the few onlookers along the road, raised their weapons over their heads, and shouted 'Allah Akhbar!'—God is great![1]

At Khafji about thirty Iraqis had been killed and another thirty-seven wounded. The Saudis suffered eighteen dead and twenty-nine wounded. During the fighting an American A-10 jet accidentally destroyed a Marine light-armored vehicle, killing eleven Marines. These casualties marked the first United States combat deaths on the ground.

The battle at Khafji, which Saddam Hussein had bragged was the start of a massive assault on Saudi Arabia, instead caused doubt about the quality of Iraqi soldiers. "We are very proud," exclaimed the commander of a Qatari tank unit. "This was the first time our army has seen combat and we have been victorious."

Saudi General Khalid added, "The morale of my troops after this fight is just great."

G-Day

On Friday, February 22, 1991, President Bush set a deadline of 12:00 P.M. the next day for Iraq to begin its withdrawal from Kuwait or risk a ground war. Saddam Hussein refused to budge. For the coalition forces, the waiting was nearly over. G-Day was here. At 4:00 A.M.

on February 24, the allies launched the ground offensive to liberate Kuwait.

That rainy morning, forward units of the U.S. 2nd Marine Division approached the first Iraqi defensive line. Overhead the sky was black with soot from huge fires, set by Iraqi soldiers, in Kuwait's al-Wafrah oil field. In front of the Marines lay huge rows of barbed wire, coils and coils strung atop one another, rigged with booby traps and mines. High barriers of sand (called "berms"), tank traps, trenches, and forts blocked the way. Marine artillerymen began the attack by firing 155-mm howitzer rounds on enemy positions. Then in a cold rain and darkness the first Marines crossed into Kuwait. Cobra helicopters whirred overhead, while M-60 tanks rolled forward. In armored vehicles and humvees, thousands of troops followed.

The 2nd Marine Division engineers approached the first Iraqi mine field, cut into the barbed wire, and fired several rocket-propelled explosive charges. These explosives are known as mine-clearing line charges, or "Mic-Lics." The exploded Mic-Lics cleared paths 300 feet (91 meters) long and 12 feet (4 meters) wide. Tanks with plows, rakes, and rollers on their fronts charged through these gaps. The engineers swiftly cut six narrow lanes through the minefields. Through those long lanes poured the entire 8,000 vehicles and 19,000 men of the 2nd Marine Division.

Marine Sergeant Don Griffin watched the engineers clear two of the breach lanes and counted four tank-plows damaged as they blew up mines. One tank was lifted right off the ground by an explosion. Ahead Iraqi mortar crews and riflemen began firing. Marine squads crawled and ran toward the Iraqis.

"We laid down a base of fire," Corporal James Disbro remembered, "and they were firing at us, and I started thinking 'Where's the air support they promised us?' I was waiting for planes to come in and bomb them."[2] Twenty minutes later, a Marine Cobra helicopter began spraying the hill in front of Disbro with machine-gun fire. Medevac helicopters hovered overhead to evacuate wounded Marines.

By 9:30 A.M. on G-Day, the 2nd and 1st Marine Divisions, together with the Army's 2nd Armored Division, were achieving a breakthrough into Kuwait. "I don't think they saw us comin'," Army tank gunner Kevin Green explained. "Then, when we hit the first [Iraqi] tanks, the other crews jumped off and ran."

"We just went up the battlefield and killed everything in our path," added Marine tank captain Roy Bierwirth. "The Abrams [tank] was just a wonderful piece of equipment."

The advancing Marines passed mines of every sort lying scattered on the ground. They saw Iraqi trenches and tanks dug in with their guns pointed at them. Other Iraqi tanks burned in flames. The Marines encountered little resistance. Some Iraqi soldiers rose cautiously out of sandy ditches and holes. They walked toward the Marines through the drizzle, offering to surrender. Many were wounded or so weak from lack of food and water that they could hardly stand.

A U.S. Marine M-60 tank with a plow attached cuts its way through a sand barrier. Tanks like this one led the charge into Kuwait on G-Day, February 24, 1991.

"The Saudis on the beach road were making remarkable progress," recalled General Schwarzkopf. "They drove past miles of abandoned bunkers and trenches before running into any resistance at all, and they also reported hundreds of Iraqis waving white flags."[3]

By the end of G-Day, the first day of the ground war, the 2nd Marine Division had destroyed four Iraqi brigades and captured roughly 5,000 prisoners. The 1st Marine Division had ripped through the Iraqi breaches and battled through the Al Burgan oil field south of Kuwait City. The retreating Iraqis had set the Kuwaiti oil fields on fire. More than 500 blazing wells belched black smoke.

Marine Colonel Hal Hornburg exclaimed, "It looks like what I envision hell would look like . . . the country of Kuwait is burning." At high noon, troops in the 1st Marine Division could see only ten feet (three meters) in any direction and had to read their maps by flashlights. The soot and oil covered their clothing and burned their throats.

On February 25, the second day of ground warfare (G + 1) in Kuwait, fighting continued at the Al Jabr airfield just west of Kuwait City. By 10:00 A.M. Marine AH-1W Sea Cobra helicopters joined in the battle. They swiftly helped knock out thirty tanks and armored personnel carriers. The helicopters hovered so close to the ground during the fight that Marines could reach up and touch the helicopter skids. Other Allied aircraft crisscrossed the sky. Despite the black smoke from the oil field fires, the rain, and the fog, 144 sturdy A-10 Warthog ground-attack jets destroyed many Iraqi tanks. Naval and land-based artillery and rockets rained down on Iraqi positions.

Along the Kuwait coast, the Marines and Saudis fought off three heavy Iraqi counterattacks. The Marines destroyed dozens of Iraqi tanks, while suffering only one dead and eighteen wounded. The Saudis and other coalition Arabs seized all of their objectives along the coast road. Huge numbers of Iraqi prisoners were marched to the rear. The coalition forces so far had achieved complete success.

The American A-10 Thunderbolt II was more commonly known as the "Warthog" because of its ugly appearance. The sturdy jet was designed to destroy tanks and other ground targets with its missiles. Sadly, during the fighting at Khafji, an A-10 accidentally blew up an American light armored vehicle, killing eleven Marines.

The "Hail Mary" Play

A key part of General Schwarzkopf's battle plan was to be a surprise flank attack where the Iraqis were weakest. "When we took out [Saddam's] air force," Schwarzkopf later recalled, "for all intents and purposes, we took out his ability to see what we were doing . . . in Saudi Arabia. Once we had taken out his eyes, we did what could be described as the 'Hail Mary' play in football. . . . we did a massive movement of troops all the way out to the west, to the extreme west. . . ."

Beginning on January 17, 1991, Schwarzkopf secretly sent two corps—the XVIII Airborne Corps and the armor-heavy VII Corps—moving westward. More than 250,000 troops, including the British 1st Armoured Division and the French 6th Light Armored Division, took part in the shift. ". . . the Army was on the move, relocating in preparation for the ground attack . . ." recalled Schwarzkopf. "By the end of the first day of the [air] war, the convoy stretched 120 miles [193 kilometers]."

In the space of about fourteen days the XVIII Airborne Corps moved 117,844 troops, 22,884 wheeled vehicles, and 5,145 tracked vehicles an average of 530 miles (853 kilometers) down a single road from its defensive to its pre-attack positions. "Not only did we move the troops out there," Schwarzkopf later declared, "but we literally moved thousands and thousands of tons of fuel, of ammunition, of spare parts, of water, and of food . . . so . . . if we got into a slugfest battle . . . we'd have enough supplies to last for sixty days. It was an absolute

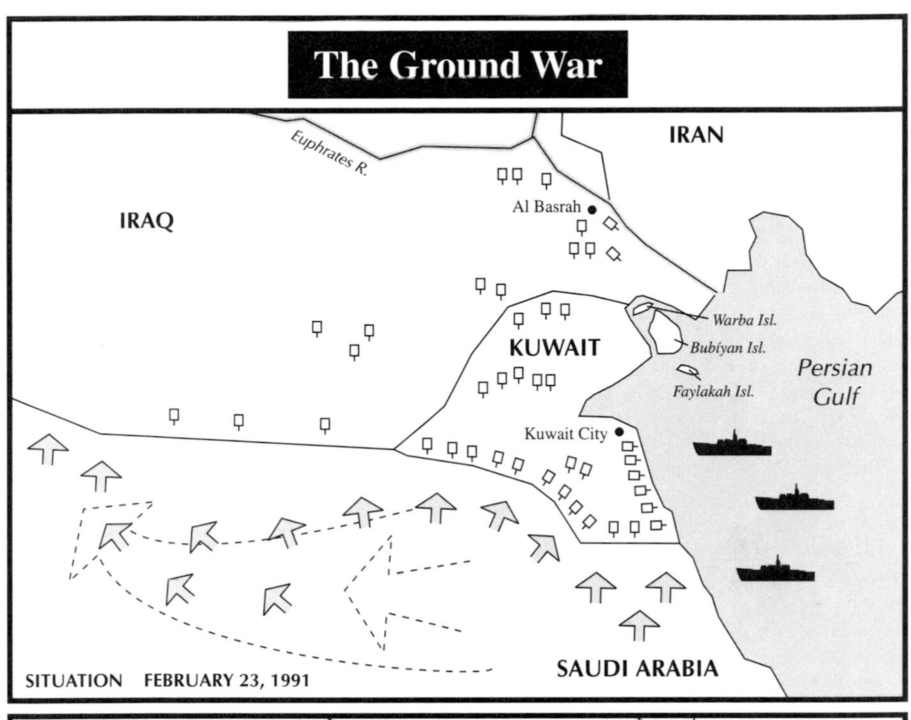
The Ground War
IRAN
Euphrates R.
IRAQ
Al Basrah
KUWAIT
Warba Isl.
Bubíyan Isl.
Persian Gulf
Faylakah Isl.
Kuwait City
SAUDI ARABIA
SITUATION FEBRUARY 23, 1991

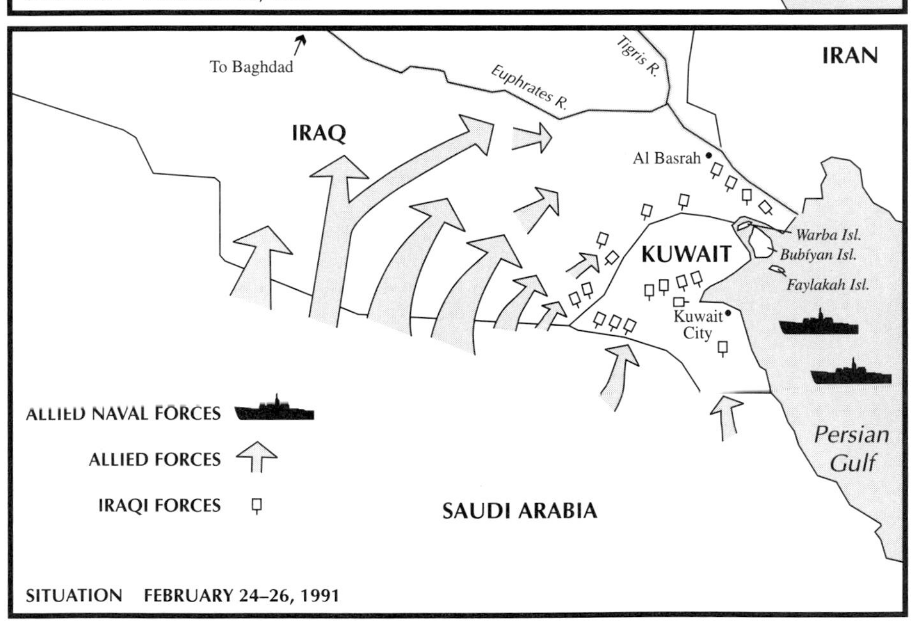
To Baghdad
Tigris R.
IRAN
Euphrates R.
IRAQ
Al Basrah
KUWAIT
Warba Isl.
Bubíyan Isl.
Faylakah Isl.
Kuwait City
Persian Gulf
ALLIED NAVAL FORCES
ALLIED FORCES
IRAQI FORCES
SAUDI ARABIA
SITUATION FEBRUARY 24–26, 1991

gigantic accomplishment. . . ."[4] No army in the history of warfare had ever moved so much so far so fast!

To keep the attention of the Iraqis focused on Kuwait, the coalition used trickery. For weeks, U.S. Marines aboard ships in the Persian Gulf "rehearsed" an assault on the beaches of Kuwait. As a result Saddam worriedly built up Kuwaiti coastal defenses and reinforced his troops there.

Instead on G-Day, February 24, the XVIII Airborne Corps, commanded by U.S. Lieutenant General Gary E. Luck, charged into the open desert of western Iraq. The armored cars of the French 6th Light Armored Division bounced across miles of rocky desert into Iraq. Along with a brigade of paratroopers from the U.S. 82nd Airborne Division, they were to seize the Al Salman air base.

The French 6th Light Armored Division possessed two tank regiments equipped with AMX-10RCs—small, fast, six-wheeled vehicles with 105-mm guns. "They just flew," exclaimed Colonel Bob Kee, an American officer traveling with the French forces. "They can go 50 miles [81 kilometers] an hour, and at times they were going that fast." The French division and the American paratroopers dashed into Iraq and drove 94 miles (151 kilometers) north. At Al Salman they smashed Iraq's 45th Infantry Division.

Thirty miles (forty-eight kilometers) east of the French and 82nd Airborne advance, the U.S. 101st Airborne Division (Air Assault) launched the largest helicopter assault in history. More than 300 Apache, Cobra, Black

Hawk, Huey, and Chinook helicopters, piloted by men and women, transported fifty miles (eighty-one kilometers) into Iraq an entire brigade of 2,000 men, including its humvees, howitzers, and tons of fuel and ammunition. There they set up a huge supply base called Forward Operations Base Cobra. The soldiers of the 101st next pushed on into the Euphrates River Valley. They cut all traffic and communications lines along a section of Highway 8, the six-lane highway connecting the southern Iraqi city of Basra with Baghdad.

The coalition forces were moving with remarkable

American troops await their orders to move across the desert into Iraq. On February 24, 1991, General Schwarzkopf unleashed his flank attack, the surprise "Hail Mary" play.

speed across great distances. Desert Storm commanders rested during breaks that lasted only a few minutes, or at most an hour or two. Troops strung hammocks inside their tanks and armored vehicles, or slept sitting up during brief pauses in the march. "It was just like a parade," one officer remarked. "The only problem was the weather."

On the second day of the war, a sandstorm prevented troops from seeing beyond one hundred feet (thirty meters). Once again superior technology aided Schwarzkopf's forces. Using handy navigation devices called "global positioning systems," coalition forces

Always on the alert, a machine gunner with the U.S. 2nd Marine Division scans the horizon from the back of a truck during the ground attack into Kuwait.

always knew exactly where they were and where they were heading.

As part of the XVIII Airborne Corps, the U.S. 24th Infantry Division also struck camp on G-Day. Within hours, a long snake-like column of M1A1 Abrams tanks and Bradley fighting vehicles moved out along three main routes of attack. "Our mission," Commanding Major General Barry McCaffrey told his troops, "is to attack 300 kilometers [186 miles] into Iraq to block the Euphrates River Valley. Our objective is to close the escape route for 500,000 enemy soldiers in Kuwait."

The 24th Division raced more than sixty miles (ninety-seven kilometers) into Iraq before meeting a single enemy soldier. Even then, the enemy was always looking the wrong way. "Never once did we attack an enemy force that saw us coming or was dug in prepared to defend against our attack," revealed Major General McCaffrey. "They were unaware we were there and they were looking the wrong way." General Schwarzkopf's "Hail Mary" play was unfolding according to plan.

Tanks Across the Sand

Just before 12:00 P.M. on February 24, General Schwarzkopf learned that Iraqi troops were abandoning Kuwait City. "So I gave the order to my forces," he recalled, "Khalid gave the order to his, and at three that afternoon we let loose the main attack of Desert Storm."

The huge VII Corps was stationed at the center of the allied line along the Iraqi border. Now General Schwarzkopf ordered the VII Corps forward,

M1A1 Abrams tanks off the U.S. 3rd Armored Division roar across the desert. As part of Lieutenant General Frederick M. Frank's VII Corps, they surged into Iraq on February 25, 1991.

ahead of schedule. The VII Corps commander Lieutenant General Frederick M. Franks immediately began issuing orders. At 3:30 P.M. on February 25, the U.S. 1st Infantry Division attacked. It breached a mine field on the Saudi-Iraqi border about 80 miles (129 kilometers) west of Kuwait and surged into Iraq. Alongside it came the U.S. 2nd Armored Cavalry Regiment. Behind them, the massed tanks of the 1st British Armored Division and the U.S. 1st and 3rd Armored Divisions charged.

Mine plows and engineer vehicles rolled forward. They cut eight lanes through the Iraqi minefields, then headed for the Iraqi trenches. When they reached the trenches, they rolled right over them. Stunned Iraqi soldiers scattered. Some came out waving flags, while others fired shots at the tanks and then surrendered. The tanks turned left and right, rolling along the side of the trenches, plowing them under. Iraqis who chose not to surrender were plowed under too. "We started taking prisoners," declared Sergeant First Class Dale Orndorf. "Then we started not taking prisoners. There were so many. We'd throw them some water and MREs and keep going."[5]

Pushing north, one Army squad encountered two Iraqi military trucks. Iraqi soldiers jumped out waving their rifles. The Americans began firing. "Everybody's shooting," Sergeant Jason Davis recalled, "and we're being shot at. Bullets are going everywhere." When several Iraqis tried to circle behind the American squad, Davis bravely stood up and stopped them with rifle fire.

The VII Corps could not be stopped. Troops

scarcely rested as they pressed ahead. At coalition command headquarters in Riyadh, reporters asked General Schwarzkopf his next plans, "Are you going to go around or over?"

Schwarzkopf bluntly replied, "We're going to go around, over, through, on top, underneath, and any other way it takes to get in."

"The Iraqi forces are conducting the Mother of all Retreats."

—U.S. Secretary of Defense Dick Cheney,
February 27, 1991

6 The 100-Hour War

The UN coalition forces sliced into Iraq and Kuwait. To meet their military goals, United States troops grimly battled every Iraqi unit that stood in their way.

Cutting Highway 8

The 24th Infantry Division (Mechanized), commanded by Major General Barry McCaffrey, boasted nearly 25,000 soldiers, 241 M1A1 Abrams tanks, 221 Bradley fighting vehicles, 72 self-propelled howitzers, 9 Multiple Launch Rocket System launchers, 18 Apache attack helicopters, and 6,000 wheeled vehicles. On the third day of the ground war, February 26, 1991, the 24th Infantry Division was still driving north. Its objective was to reach Highway 8 and take control, reinforcing the 2,000 men of Major General Binford Peay's 101st Airborne Division.

Advancing deeper into Iraq, McCaffrey's soldiers scattered Iraqi positions with rockets and long-range artillery—completely surprising the enemy. "They had no earthly idea where it was coming from," remarked Colonel John Le Moyne. The 24th Division completed its dash into the Euphrates River Valley by sundown on February 26. By using their night-vision sights, gunners on the M1A1 Abrams tanks spotted Iraqi T-72 tanks at far greater ranges than the Iraqis could see them. The 24th Division captured the towns of Tallil and Jaliba and overran a large supply dump and two air-fields. Then it turned eastward down Highway 8 toward Basra.

Lieutenant Colonel B. J. Craddock commanded a battalion of the 24th Division. His companies reached Highway 8 about 6:00 P.M. He placed his mechanized company astride the six-lane thoroughfare, with two tank companies in front. Iraqis fleeing north from Basra in military trucks and armored-vehicle transporters had no idea that the Americans were there.

The American tankers surprised and fought Republican Guard units from the Al Faw, Adnan, and Nebuchadnezzar Divisions. "They would just roll right in, 50 to 100 trucks, and they kept coming," Lieutenant Colonel Craddock explained. "There were heavy equipment transporters with armored vehicles on them. Great landmarks. Those things burned all night long."[1]

U.S. tanks hold Highway 8. On February 26, 1991, M1A1 Abrams tanks of the 24th Infantry Division (Mechanized) captured sections of the vital Iraqi highway. The coalition's dash into the Euphrates River Valley surprised the Iraqis completely.

Battling the Republican Guard

". . . the long-term success of Desert Storm was now riding on VII Corps," declared General Schwarzkopf. "I was confident they could destroy the Republican Guard—if only they could get there before the war ended."

During the first full day of coalition ground attacks, three Republican Guard divisions—the Tawakalna, the Medina Luminous, and the Hammurabi—had not moved. They remained positioned to the southwest of the city of Basra. Each contained at least 13,000 men and 350 Soviet T-72 tanks.

The VII Corps was still pushing north from the center of the coalition battle line. Now Lieutenant General Franks ordered the 1st and 3rd U.S. Armored Divisions and the 1st Infantry Division, with more than 1,000 tanks and 50,000 soldiers, to halt their northward drive and wheel to the east, charging toward Saddam's elite force. At the same time Franks ordered the British 1st Armored Division to turn due east toward Kuwait. This would make four, full, heavy-armored divisions smashing at the Iraqi forces south of Basra and inside Kuwait. One of the largest tank battles in history was about to begin.

Late on the third day of the ground war, February 26, two United States armored cavalry units—Captain Gerald Davie's troop with the 3rd Armored Division and Captain H. R. McMaster's troop with the 2nd Armored Cavalry Regiment—hit the Iraqi line. McMaster's Eagle Troop contained 140 soldiers, 9 M1A1 Abrams main battle tanks, 12 Bradley fighting vehicles, 2 4.2-inch mortar carriers as well as support and transport vehicles. On either side of McMaster other troops of the 2nd Armored Cavalry Regiment—named Ghost, Iron, Killer, Bull, and Apache—were similarly equipped.

Through a heavy desert sandstorm, McMaster's tank crested a slight rise. Suddenly McMaster's gunner Staff Sergeant Craig Koch yelled, "Tanks, direct front!" Just ahead, dug in and protected by large mounds of dirt, stood eight Iraqi tanks from the Tawakalna Division of the Republican Guard. Quickly Staff Sergeant Koch pushed the button on his laser range-finder. The display

Direct hit! Sparks and metal spray into the air as an Iraqi tank explodes. On the night of February 26-27, 1991, tanks of the coalition's VII Corps smashed units of Iraq's famed Republican Guard. It was perhaps the largest tank battle in history.

beneath the red crosshairs showed that the tank stood exactly 4,658 feet (1,420 meters) away. "Fire," McMaster ordered. Koch pulled the trigger, and the enemy tank exploded in a fireball.

Koch swung the crosshairs onto another Iraqi tank. Beneath him, the tank's loader Private Jeffrey Taylor grabbed an explosive round from the ready-rack and slammed it into the breech. "Up!" he yelled. The gun was loaded and ready for firing. Koch squeezed the trigger again. The smashed turret of an enemy tank popped into the air in a sudden explosion of sparks.

The rest of the tanks of McMaster's Eagle Troop crested the ridge, and gunners hurriedly picked their targets. The rest of the Iraqi tanks burst into flames. Eagle Troop pushed forward, cutting through the Tawakalna Division, destroying T-72 tanks and Iraqi armored vehicles.

Davie's company of Bradley fighting vehicles had a much tougher time. As it pushed into the Tawakalna Division it suddenly faced T-72 tanks and artillery units. "We didn't know how badly we were into it," Davie later recalled. "At that point, we were really just fighting for our lives."

Two soldiers—Staff Sergeant Kenneth Gentry and Sergeant Edwin Kutz—died in the fighting.

"There was a lot of metal flying around," Davie explained. Twelve of Davie's Bradleys were hit by Iraqi artillery rounds, shrapnel, small-arms fire, or worse. Of the thirty-six Purple Hearts awarded to the killed and wounded soldiers of the 3rd Armored Division, fourteen would go to the men in Davie's troop.

Soldiers of the 1st Infantry Division also smashed into the enemy through the night and into the morning of February 27. Side by side the tanks drove east, firing into the Iraqi lines. Cannon boomed and flashed, and the red tracers of the shells streaked through the night. The men watched the turrets of Iraqi tanks explode and ammunition go rocketing into the air. The Americans destroyed enemy T-72 tanks, T-59 tanks, armored fighting vehicles, anti-aircraft guns, and trucks. They hit a bunker filled with 155-mm artillery ammunition, which exploded with a startling blast.

The U.S. 3rd Armored Division and the British 1st Armored Division joined in, destroying other Iraqi infantry and armored units. "Not surprisingly the Republican Guard fought hard to hold their ground," recalled General Schwarzkopf. "But we overwhelmed them and by dawn our reports showed that the Tawakalna Division had been almost completely destroyed while we hadn't lost a single tank."[2]

At first light on February 27, the U.S. 1st Armored Division continued moving forward, its tanks spaced ninety-eight feet (thirty meters) apart. The division stretched in a line fifteen miles (twenty-four kilometers) wide across the desert. Nothing could stop these tanks from cutting off the retreat of Saddam's army through northern Kuwait.

In the early afternoon the 2nd Brigade of the 1st Armored Division attacked the Iraqi Medina Luminous

An Iraqi T-55 tank burns in the desert. It was destroyed by a tank of the British 1st Armoured Division, part of the coalition's VII Corp's advance.

Division, which was dug in along a slope. The American tankers later called this the Battle of Medina Ridge—the largest tank battle of the Gulf War.

"Fire," tank commanders shouted. "On the way," answered their gunners. The guns boomed, the breeches kicked back, and the smell of gunpowder filled each tank. Specialist Shannon Boldman worked as a gunner on one M1A1 tank. "I just kept going from target to target," he recalled, "left to right. And it was just like, there's another tank, 'Shoot it', boom, there's another one, 'Shoot it', boom. That was how it went."

In forty minutes the 2nd Brigade destroyed sixty Iraqi T-72 tanks, nine T-55 tanks, thirty-eight armored personnel carriers, and five SA-13 air-defense guns. About 340 Iraqi soldiers were killed in the fight, and another 55 were taken prisoner.

During the afternoon the weather cleared. Then Apache helicopters swooped down on enemy targets. The pilots unleashed their laser-guided Hellfire anti-tank missiles, 2.75-inch rockets, and 30-mm guns. They watched little white dots explode on the ground as Iraqi tanks blew up. One company of Apaches knocked out an additional thirty tanks belonging to the Medina Luminous Division.

Iraqi survivors fled into a defensive area south of Basra and north of Kuwait that would become called the "Basra pocket." But the VII Corps had dealt a terrible blow to the enemy. "We killed 630 tanks and only lost 4 tanks and 2 Bradleys," declared General Ronald Griffith, commander of the American 1st Division. "I don't think there is any doubt that we destroyed the Republican Guard."

Tragedy and Triumph

At 8:20 P.M. on February 26, 1991, U.S. Army Specialist Ruben Carranzas was resting on his cot in a converted water-bottling plant at Al Khobar near Dhahran, Saudi Arabia. The large barracks building had a concrete floor. Steel beams reinforced its concrete walls. A few yards away from Carranzas, fellow members of the 14th Quartermaster Detachment talked, laughed, and relaxed. The 14th Quartermaster Detachment was a reserve unit from Greensburg, Pennsylvania. The unit had arrived in Saudi Arabia just one week earlier. Its mission was to assist other units with water purification.

At 8:23 P.M. pieces of an Iraqi Scud missile suddenly crashed through the barracks roof. "I got blown out of my bunker about twenty feet [six meters] . . ." Carranzas remembered. "I felt blood gushing out of my ear. Shrapnel covered my face. I couldn't see anything. My face was covered with blood. I could hear people screaming and crying out for help."

Private Anthony Drees from North Dakota recalled hearing a boom and snap. "I knew I'd been hit," he later exclaimed. "I caught my breath for a second and looked, and the whole building was gone. My bunk was against the wall and it was gone. I reached back and pieces of my leg were missing. My right shoe was off. I tried to chase it around and I couldn't. My friend next to me had both legs blown off."[3]

Little remained of the barracks at Al Khobar, Saudi Arabia after pieces of an Iraqi Scud missile struck it on February 26, 1991. The horrible blast killed 28 American troops and wounded 100 others.

Some soldiers lay crushed under concrete rubble. Others suffered terrible burns. Altogether 28 Americans died and another 100 were wounded. The shocking blast caused the largest number of coalition casualties from a single attack in Operation Desert Storm.

The Iraqi troops suffered far greater casualties as they tried to escape Kuwait. Driving west of Kuwait City, the U.S. Army's 2nd Armored Division, nicknamed the Tiger Brigade, encountered enemy vehicles on the highway. Within five minutes, the Tiger Brigade destroyed twenty Iraqi tanks. "That was what we call a counterattack, because it makes us feel better," Colonel John Sylvester remarked afterward. "I'm not sure whether it was a counterattack, or whether it was twenty tanks trying to get the hell out of Dodge."

The Tiger Brigade eventually took control of the Mutlah Ridge. The Americans gazed beyond at a shocking scene of destruction. Where the highway passed through the Mutlah Ridge, they saw hundreds of blackened and burned-out vehicles. The previous night, U.S. Marine and Air Force aircraft had blown them up. It was a three-mile-long (5-kilometer-long) ruin of abandoned, burned, and wrecked trucks, buses, jeeps, cars, and armored personnel carriers. Many were loaded with loot from Kuwait City—carpets, furniture, televisions, videocassette recorders, clothing, shoes, perfume, cigarettes, and various other items. In some vehicles charred bodies could be seen. The road between the Mutlah Pass northwest of Kuwait City, Kuwait, and Basra, Iraq, soon became known to the world as the "Highway of Death."

The Tiger Brigade's assignment was to cut off all additional fleeing Iraqi forces. *Newsweek* magazine reporter Tony Clifton traveled with the lead tanks of the "Hounds of Hell" Battalion. Clifton described his experience:

> We reached our main objective at about 4:00 P.M. Wednesday. The al-Mutlaa police station . . . west of Kuwait City on the main Sixth Ring Motorway, which turns into the highway north to Iraq. We couldn't see it clearly, but thousands of Iraqis were trying to escape up the highway. . . . In the smoky twilight, the lead tanks opened

At the Mutlah Pass outside Kuwait City, battered vehicles litter the road which became known as the "Highway of Death." U.S. aircraft and tanks destroyed everything that moved, as the Iraqis tried to flee northward. "Our orders were to stop them," grimly recalled one American soldier. "And stop them we did."

> up. . . . An Iraqi T-55 tank immediately blew up in a great fountain of white fire. . . . Next to go was an armored personnel carrier. Then a line of fuel tankers spewed flame and oily smoke across the other burning vehicles. Orange and green tracers swept the buildings and armored vehicles now scattering off the road. . . . Apart from military vehicles of all kinds, there were private Kuwaiti automobiles, Kuwaiti police cars, orange school buses, trucks and ambulances. . . . Nearly all were piled with loot.

"Well, our orders were to stop them" remembered one American soldier. "And stop them we did. Every one of 'em. It was our last action of Desert Storm. . . ."

Along an overall battle line stretching 300 miles (483 kilometers), the beaten Iraqis were surrendering. Masses of them, bewildered and hungry, were marching across the desert toward the allies. Altogether about 65,000 Iraqi soldiers were taken prisoner during the war. One American pilot was forced to eject and land in the desert. He soon found himself surrounded by dozens of Iraqi troops trying to surrender to him. Elsewhere an American humvee became separated from its column and got stuck in the mud. An Iraqi tank appeared, towed the humvee out, and then surrendered to the Americans. "You'd come over the ridges," declared Colonel Ron Rokosz of the 82nd Airborne Division, "and they'd be coming out of their holes, waving a white flag all over the place; it was the most incredible thing I've ever seen."

Kuwait Is Liberated

"We certainly did not expect it to go this way," remarked General Schwarzkopf. The fight to free Kuwait moved faster and with greater success than anyone could have imagined.

By day's end on February 27, U.S. Marine and Arab forces in Kuwait had destroyed Iraq's 3rd Armored Division, liberated the Kuwait airport, and taken control of the roads into Kuwait City. Iraqi troops were

Beaten and weary, Iraqi troops trudge across the sand to surrender. Army lieutenant Mark Eichelman advanced into Kuwait with the tanks of the American Tiger Brigade. Everywhere he looked "Iraqis ran out waving their white flags, their hands up." As many as 65,000 Iraqi troops became prisoners during the war.

fleeing north, pursued by coalition units and attacked relentlessly from the air. In three and one-half days of sharp fighting, more than 29 Iraqi divisions were smashed, with an estimated 3,000 tanks destroyed or captured.

The 1st and 2nd U.S. Marine Divisions advanced to the outskirts of Kuwait City and then pulled to the side of the roadways. Kuwaiti, Saudi, Egyptian, and other Arab forces in the coalition received the actual honor of liberating the Kuwaiti capital. One journalist wrote: "Columns of Kuwaiti and Saudi tanks and personnel carriers rumbled up the broad boulevards of Kuwait City, passed barbed wire and bunkers, burnt-out tanks and wrecked cars, and freed the battered capital." *Time* magazine reporter Bruce W. Nelan observed:

> On February 27, six months and 25 days after Iraqi tanks crushed Kuwait beneath their treads, another column of armored vehicles rumbled into the capital city . . . civilian cars formed a convoy around them, horns honking, flags waving. Crowds along the way danced and chanted, "Allah akbar!", "U.S.A.! U.S.A.!", and "Thank you, thank you!" Thousands swarmed onto the streets, embracing and kissing the arriving soldiers. . . . Everywhere the green, white, red, and black Kuwaiti flag, which had been outlawed during the occupation, fluttered from buildings, bridges and hats. . . . A woman in black robes blew kisses at U.S. Marine Lieutenant General Walt Boomer, who rode atop one of the troop carriers. "We'll never see anything like this

Kuwait is liberated! Waving their national flag, Kuwaiti children joined the celebration in Kuwait City. Grinning civilians hugged coalition soldiers in the streets. Seven months of Iraqi occupation was at an end.

> again in our lifetime," Boomer declared. "Makes you appreciate freedom, doesn't it?"[4]

At the White House in Washington, D.C., President Bush, Secretary of Defense Cheney, General Powell, and other top advisors discussed the military situation. Soon Powell telephoned General Schwarzkopf and asked if Schwarzkopf thought a cease-fire would now be appropriate. Schwarzkopf would have liked a few more hours to destroy the remaining enemy units trying to escape to Basra. He agreed, however, when President Bush finally decided to order the cease-fire.

At 2:30 A.M. on February 28, Major General Barry McCaffrey walked out of the temporary tent headquarters of the 24th Infantry Division. "It's all over," he announced to his staff. "They've told us to hold in place. A cease-fire is scheduled to take effect at 8:00 A.M."

". . . the time had come to stop the fighting," President Bush later remarked. "The goal was to kick Iraq out of Kuwait, and the goal . . . had been achieved." Coalition forces fully controlled Kuwait and occupied one-fifth of Iraq.

In an address to the world, President Bush proclaimed:

> Kuwait is liberated. Iraq's army is defeated. Our military objectives are met. . . . After consulting with Secretary of Defense Cheney, Chairman of the Joint Chiefs of Staff Powell, and our coalition partners, I am pleased to announce that . . . exactly one hundred hours since ground operations commenced and six weeks since the

> start of Operation Desert Storm, all United States and Coalition Forces will suspend offensive combat operations.[5]

Iraqi Foreign Minister Tariq Aziz soon dispatched a letter to the UN Security Council. The letter promised that Iraq would comply with all UN resolutions. Saddam also accepted Bush's demand for a meeting of military commanders to discuss terms for an unconditional surrender. Some reporters asked General Schwarzkopf if the coalition forces should have gone all the way to Baghdad. "We were 150 miles [242 kilometers] away from Baghdad," responded the general, "and there was nobody between us and Baghdad. If it had been our intention to take Iraq . . . we could have done it unopposed. . . . But that was not our intention. . . . Our intention was purely to eject the Iraqis out of Kuwait and to destroy [Iraq's] military power. . . ."

"As Commander in Chief, I can report to you: Our armed forces fought with honor and valor. And as President, I can report to the nation aggression is defeated. The war is over."

—President George Bush in an address to Congress, March 6, 1991

7 The Aftermath

At 11:30 A.M. on March 3, 1991, General H. Norman Schwarzkopf and Saudi Lieutenant General Khalid bin Sultan took seats at a long table inside a large tent at Safwan Air-Field in southern Iraq. Across the table sat Iraqi Lieutenant General Sultan Hashim Ahmad and his aide Lieutenant General Salah Abud Mahumd. Schwarzkopf calmly told the Iraqi generals the terms of the cease-fire. The Iraqi forces must stop resisting.

President Bush's cease-fire announcement on February 27 had not been honored by the Iraqis. On March 2, Republican Guard troops of the Hammurabi Division tried to withdraw up the Euphrates River Valley. A large tank battle erupted when these Iraqis fired upon blocking units of the U.S. 24th Infantry Division. In a fight that lasted several hours, the 24th Division destroyed eighty-one Iraqi tanks, ninety-five armored personnel carriers, eleven battlefield missile systems, and twenty-three trucks. "We brought the sky in on the Iraqis," declared one XVIII Corps officer.[1]

At the Safwan cease-fire meeting, the Iraqis agreed to all terms. The Persian Gulf War ended. In the fighting, United States forces had suffered 148 troops killed in action and 339 wounded, plus 10 more missing. Among the coalition partners, two French and ten British soldiers

At Safwan Airfield, Iraq, General H. Norman Schwarzkopf (seated at left) meets with Iraqi generals to discuss cease-fire terms. Coalition partner Lieutenant General Khalid bin-Sultan of Saudi Arabia sits at Schwarzkopf's left.

were killed. Casualties in the allied Arab units were equally light. An estimated 100,000 Iraqi soldiers died in the lopsided fighting. The number of Kuwaitis tortured and murdered during the Iraqi occupation was estimated to be in the thousands.

The war left Iraq in turmoil. Southern Iraq was a stronghold of Iraq's Shiite Muslim sect. In the war's aftermath, they hoped to grab political control from the Sunni Muslims of the Baathist Party. Shiite Muslims took to the streets and battled Republican Guard units. Shiite rebels captured dozens of Iraqi towns, burning police stations and killing many local Baathist leaders. But Saddam fought back, making major cities such as Basra, Najaf, and Karbala bloody battlegrounds. The Republican Guard ruthlessly sent its remaining tanks and artillery against its own people. Thousands of Shiite civilians died in massacres.

To the north, Iraqi Kurds also revolted against Saddam. Saddam's troops swiftly counterattacked. Iraqi helicopters flew low over Kurdish villages, firing on citizens and dropping explosives. More than one million Kurds fled their war-torn villages. On foot, by mule, by truck, and by car, they headed for refuge across the borders of Turkey and Iran. In filthy mountain camps, the very young and the very old began dying of starvation and disease at the rate of 1,000 a day.

On April 11, 1991, President Bush announced a major United States relief effort for the more than 500,000 Iraqi Kurds in Turkey. Parachutes dropped food and clothing on the refugee camps. Over 10,000 American

Iraqi soldiers set more than 500 Kuwaiti oil wells ablaze during the war. The thick, black smoke caused an ecological disaster, as millions of gallons of oil burned each day.

troops joined with British, French, and Dutch forces, giving protection to the refugees, building tent camps, and urging the Kurds to return in safety to their villages.

Ecologically, Kuwait suffered more from the Persian Gulf War than did Iraq. The wreckage of thousands of burnt-out tanks and armored vehicles littered the Kuwaiti desert. In Kuwait City stood the ruins of buildings, destroyed by allied bombing or Iraqi vandalism. Along the roads lay smashed tanks, crumpled trailers, severed electricity cables, and upturned vehicles. In addition there were thousands of unexploded mines, booby traps, and other explosives that had to be cleared. The job of disarming or exploding the land mines required time and patience.

Kuwait's oil fields remained ablaze for months. Retreating Iraqi soldiers had set fire to more than 500 oil wells. Some five million gallons of oil a day were going up in flames. Black choking smoke blotted out the sun. Breathing, declared a Kuwaiti, was "like taking the exhaust pipe of a diesel truck in your mouth and breathing that."[2]

First the oil fields had to be cleared of unexploded mines. Then workers dug pipelines for the tons of seawater the firefighters needed to cool the burning wellheads. Firefighters drilled diagonal relief walls and filled the wells with mud or cement. This capping process cost as much as $10 million per well. Many millions of dollars later, the last fire was snuffed out in November 1991. Altogether it would cost an estimated $50 billion dollars to rebuild Kuwait and return it to its prewar condition.

Special crews of American firefighters called "hellfighters" struggle to extinguish the blaze of a Kuwaiti oil well.

Immediately after the fighting was over, the greatest concern of Americans was to see their loved ones again. On March 6, 1991, President Bush promised:

> Soon, very soon, our troops will begin the march we've all been waiting for, their march home. . . . this victory belongs to them, to the privates and the pilots, to the sergeants and the supply officers, to the men and women in the machines, and the men and women who made them work. It belongs to the regulars, to the reserves, to the national guard. This victory belongs to the finest fighting force this nation has ever known in its history.

As soon as the war ended United States troops began flying home from Saudi Arabia at the rate of several thousand per day. By late April 1991, the last United States troops were withdrawn from southern Iraq. In America, returning troops enjoyed grand celebrations and parades. In June 1991, more than 8,000 veterans of Operation Desert Storm proudly marched down Constitution Avenue in downtown Washington, D.C., during a welcome-home parade. Another big celebration occurred in New York City. Grinning United States troops marched along Broadway in a blizzard of tickertape.

"You're going to come home such a hero," a reporter told General Schwarzkopf in an interview.

Schwarzkopf corrected her. "But I'm not a hero, and that's important. . . . It doesn't take a hero to order men into battle. It takes a hero to be one of those men that goes into battle. . . . Those are the people that are the

Thousands of Americans proudly watch as United States veterans of Operation Desert Storm march past the Lincoln Memorial in Washington, D.C.

United States troops rest in Kuwait at the end of the Persian Gulf War. On behalf of freedom, they traveled halfway around the world.

heroes."[3] All of America cheered their heroes when they returned from the Persian Gulf War.

A UN peacekeeping force moved into the portion of Iraq along the Kuwait border. Iraq also agreed to the destruction of its biological and chemical weapons, and long-range missiles. The allied forces had destroyed or captured more than half of Iraq's armored personnel carriers, about three-quarters of its tanks, and more than three-quarters of its artillery. But Saddam Hussein still held command of Iraq with an estimated 25 to 27 divisions, totaling between 300,000 and 500,000 men.

In late September 1991, President Bush reminded the press: "Saddam Hussein will, in fact, one day be gone. We can only hope that that day will be soon and that the people of Iraq will have the opportunity to choose a leader who will respect them."

Saddam felt bitter personal hatred toward George Bush and sought revenge. As an ex-president, in April 1993, Bush accepted an invitation to visit Kuwait. The Iraqi Intelligence Service used the opportunity to order George Bush's murder. On April 14, 1993, Bush visited Kuwait. Luckily, just days earlier, the Kuwaiti police arrested fourteen men on suspicion of plotting a car-bomb attack. The United States responded to this assassination attempt with force. On June 27, the U.S. Navy launched twenty-three Tomahawk missiles from the destroyer U.S.S. *Peterson*, in the Red Sea, and the cruiser U.S.S. *Chancellorsville*, sailing in the Persian Gulf. The missiles completely destroyed the Iraqi Intelligence Service headquarters in Baghdad.

"The Iraqi attack against President Bush was an attack against our country, and against all Americans," President Bill Clinton stated from the Oval Office. "We could not, and have not, let such action against our nation go unanswered." Saddam Hussein had received his latest warning. Americans hoped it would not be necessary to teach him any further lessons.

The Persian Gulf War had taught the United States the military values of strategy, speed, and high technology. Most United States troops also came home with a deeper appreciation for freedom and democracy. "We went halfway around the world to do what is moral and just and right," President Bush would remind Americans. "And we fought hard, and—with others—we won the war."

Chronology

July 17, 1979—Saddam Hussein seizes power in Iraq.

September 4, 1980—Iraq begins costly eight-year war with neighboring Iran.

July 17, 1990—Hussein threatens to use force to get Iraq out of debt.

August 2, 1990—Iraqi troops invade the oil-rich nation of Kuwait; the United Nations passes Resolution 660, condemning the Iraqi invasion, and demanding immediate and unconditional withdrawal.

August 6, 1990—United Nations passes Resolution 661, calling for a trade embargo of Iraq.

August 7, 1990—U.S. President George Bush announces the start of Operation Desert Shield; United States troops head to the Persian Gulf to protect Saudi Arabia from Iraq.

August 1990–January 1991—United Nations coalition troops build up in the Persian Gulf; thirty-one nations, led by the United States, contribute more than 695,000 troops.

November 29, 1990—The United Nations passes Resolution 678, establishing a six-week deadline for Iraq to withdraw from Kuwait.

January 12, 1991—U.S. Congress passes resolution supporting the use of force, if necessary, in the Persian Gulf.

January 17, 1991—War in the air begins in the Persian Gulf; coalition aircraft and missiles attack Baghdad and other Iraqi targets at the start of Operation Desert Storm.

January 18, 1991—Iraqis launch first Scud missile attack on Israel.

January 25, 1991—Iraqis begin dumping crude oil into the Persian Gulf.

January 29, 1991—Iraqi troops capture the Saudi border town of Khafji; coalition troops recapture Khafji thirty-six hours later.

February 22, 1991—President Bush gives Saddam Hussein final deadline to withdraw from Kuwait.

February 24, 1991—War on the ground begins in the Persian Gulf; coalition troops breach enemy defenses in Kuwait; coalition troops along the western border of Iraq dash forward in surprise attacks.

February 25, 1991—U.S. Marines capture Al Jabr air-field west of Kuwait City; the U.S. VII Corps and additional coalition forces join ground attack in Iraq.

February 26, 1991—U.S. 24th Infantry Division cuts Highway 8 deep inside Iraq; the VII Corps tanks battle Iraqi Republican Guard divisions; a Scud missile strikes a United States military barracks near Dharan, Saudi Arabia, killing twenty-eight.

February 27, 1991—The VII Corps tanks defeat additional Iraqi Republican Guard units; retreating Iraqi troops attacked by coalition aircraft and tanks along the "Highway of Death" leading toward Basra, Iraq; Arab coalition forces liberate Kuwait City; President Bush announces a cease-fire.

March 3, 1991—U.S. General H. Norman Schwarzkopf meets Iraqi generals at Safwan, Iraq, to discuss cease-fire arrangements.

April 6, 1991—Iraq accepts all United Nations resolutions.

Notes by Chapter

Chapter 1

1. Robert Weiner, *Live from Baghdad.* New York: Doubleday, 1992, pp. 259–260.

2. James F. Clarity, "From TV Reporters in Iraq, News an Attack Has Begun," *New York Times* (January 17, 1991), p. A15.

3. "Excerpts From CNN Report," *New York Times* (January 17, 1991), p. A19.

4. Weiner, p. 266.

Chapter 2

1. Peter Cipkowski, *Understanding the Crisis in the Persian Gulf.* New York: John Wiley & Sons, Inc., 1992, p. 56.

2. Judith Miller and Laurie Mylroie, *Saddam Hussein and the Crisis in the Gulf.* New York: Times Books, Random House, Inc., 1990, p. 212.

3. U.S. News & World Report Staff, *Triumph Without Victory.* New York: Times Books, Random House, Inc., 1992, p. 84.

4. "Excerpts From Bush's Statement on U.S. Defense of Saudis," *New York Times* (August 9, 1990), p. A15.

5. Bill Adler, *The Generals.* New York: Avon Books, 1991, p. 19.

6. Thomas B. Allen, F. Clifton Berry, and Norman Polmar, *War in the Gulf.* Atlanta: Turner Publishing, Inc., 1991, p. 178.

Chapter 3

1. Colonel Harry G. Summers, Jr., *A Critical Analysis of the Gulf War.* New York: Dell Publishing, 1992, p. 211.

2. Thomas B. Allen, F. Clifton Berry, and Norman Polmar, *War in the Gulf.* Atlanta: Turner Publishing, Inc., 1991, pp. 164–166.

3. Roger Cohen and Claudio Gatti, *In the Eye of the Storm.* New York: Berkley Books, 1991, p. 238.

4. Tom Mathews, "Letters in the Sand," *Newsweek* (November 19, 1990), p. 28.

5. Barry McWilliams, *This Ain't Hell . . . But You Can See It From Here!* Novato, Calif.: Presidio Press, 1992, p. 12.

6. "Excerpt From Speech By Bush at Marine Post," *New York Times* (November 23, 1990), p. A16.

Chapter 4

1. Lisa Beyer, "The Battle Beckons," *Time* (October 8, 1990), p. 26.

2. Peter Cipkowski, *Understanding the Crisis in the Persian Gulf.* New York: John Wiley & Sons, Inc., 1992, p. 107.

3. General H. Norman Schwarzkopf, *It Doesn't Take a Hero.* New York: Bantam Books, 1992, p. 415.

4. Marian Salzman and Ann O'Reilly, *War and Peace in the Persian Gulf.* Princeton, N.J.: Peterson's Guides, 1991, p. 49.

5. Thomas B. Allen, F. Clifton Berry, and Norman Polmar, *War in the Gulf.* Atlanta: Turner Publishing, Inc., 1991, p. 125.

6. Barry McWilliams, *This Ain't Hell . . . But You Can See It From Here!.* Novato, Calif.: Presidio Press, 1992, p. 95.

Chapter 5

1. Chris Hedges, "Town Regained, Morale Of Arab Allies Is Lifted," *New York Times* (February 2, 1991), p. 5.

2. U.S. News & World Report Staff, *Triumph Without Victory.* New York: Times Books, Random House, Inc., 1992, p. 310.

3. General H. Norman Schwarzkopf, *It Doesn't Take a Hero.* New York: Bantam Books, 1992, pp. 452–453.

4. Bill Adler, *The Generals.* New York: Avon Books, 1991, pp. 194–195.

5. U.S. News & World Report Staff, p. 320.

Chapter 6

1. U.S. News & World Report Staff, *Triumph Without Victory.* New York: Times Books, Random House, Inc., 1992, p. 350.

2. General H. Norman Schwarzkopf, *It Doesn't Take a Hero.* New York: Bantam Books, 1992, p. 466.

3. "Wounded G.I.s Tell Of Barracks Horror When Scud Struck," *New York Times* (March 3, 1991), p. 17.

4. Bruce W. Nelan, "Free at Last! Free at Last!" *Time* (March 11, 1991), pp. 38–39.

5. Colonel Harry G. Summers, Jr., *A Critical Analysis of the Gulf War.* New York: Dell Publishing, 1992, p. 176.

Chapter 7

1. Roger Cohen and Claudio Gatti, *In the Eye of the Storm.* New York: Berkley Books, 1991, p. 317.

2. Thomas B. Allen, F. Clifton Berry, and Norman Polmar, *War in the Gulf.* Atlanta: Turner Publishing, Inc., 1991, p. 211.

3. Bill Adler, *The Generals.* New York: Avon Books, 1991, p. 214.

Further Reading

Cipkowski, Peter. *Understanding the Crisis in the Persian Gulf.* New York: John Wiley & Sons, Inc., 1992.

Foster, Leila M. *The Story of the Persian Gulf War.* Chicago: Children's Press, 1991,

Haskins, James. *Colin Powell: A Biography.* New York: Scholastic, Inc., 1992.

Kent, Zachary. *George Bush.* Chicago: Children's Press. 1993.

King, John. *The Gulf War.* New York: Macmillan Publishing Co., 1991.

Renfrew, Nita. *Saddam Hussein.* New York: Chelsea House, 1992.

Salzman. Marian, and Ann O'Reilly. *War and Peace in the Persian Gulf.* Princeton, NJ.: Peterson's Guides, 1991.

Steloff, Rebecca. *Norman Schwarzkopf.* New York: Chelsea House, 1992.

Internet Sites

XVIII Airborne Corps History Office Operation Desert Shield/ Desert Storm: Oral History Interviews
http://www.army.mil/cmh-pg/documents/swa/dsit/dsit.htm

807th MASH—Operation Desert Shield and Operation Desert Storm
http://www.iglou.com/law/mash.htm

The 1991 Air Battle for Baghdad—Washington Post
http://www.washingtonpost.com/wp-srv/inatl/longterm/fogofwar/fogofwar.htm

Desert-Storm.com
http://www.desert-storm.com/

Frontline: The Gulf War
http://www.pbs.org/wgbh/pages/frontline/gulf/index.html

The Gulf War
http://www.indepthinfo.com/iraq/index.shtml

Gulf War Debriefing Book
http://www.leyden.com/gulfwar/index.html

Gulf War Veteran Resource Page
http://www.gulfweb.org/

Operation Desert Storm
http://www.fas.org/man/dod-101/ops/desert_storm.htm

U.S. Navy in Desert Shield/Desert Storm
http://www.history.navy.mil/wars/dstorm/index.html

Index

A

Al Khobar, Saudi Arabia, 98–100
allied forces. *See* multinational forces.
America, U.S.S., 60
Arnett, Peter, 6–11
Aspell, Tom, 5
Aziz, Tariq, 53, 107

B

Baath party, 14, 110
Baghdad, Iraq, 5, 107
 air assaults on, 58–63, 117
 bombing of, 5–11
Baker, James, 53,
Basra, 36, 83, 90, 92, 97, 100, 106
Bush, George, 12
 assassination attempt on, 117
 hostages and, 23, 53
 Kuwait invasion and, 20–21, 37
 Kuwait liberation and, 58, 74, 106–107
 leadership, 49, *50*, 52, 52–53
 Saudi Arabia and, 22, 49, 50

C

Carlucci, Frank, 24
chemical and biological warfare, 34, 42, *43*, 64, 117
Cheney, Richard, 21, 26, 89, 106
Clinton, Bill, 118
CNN, 6, 11
Congress, U.S., 24, 53–54
Cox, Sir Percy, 12, 14

D

desert, 42, 45–47
Dhahran, Saudi Arabia, 30, 32, 64
 tragedy at, 98, *99*, 100

E

Eisenhower, U.S.S., 31
environmental terrorism, 66, *67*, 78, *111*
Egypt, 34
Emir of Kuwait, 18, 20

F

Fahd, King Ibn Abdel–Aziz, 21, 38
Fahd, Sheik, 18
Fitzwater, Marlin, 5

G

ground assault, beginning of, 74, *81*

H

"Hail Mary" play, 80–85
"Highway of Death," 100, *101*
Hitler, Adolf, 14
Holliman, John, 6–11
human, shields, 22–23
Hussein, Saddam, *17*
 birthplace, 14
 hostages and, 22–23, 53
 Kuwait invasion by, 12,
 leadership, 15, 16, 52, 54, 117, 118
 rise to power, 13–16
 war against, 29

I

Independence, U.S.S., 31
Iran-Iraq war, 15

Iraq
aftermath of war, 110
Arab nations and, 15–16
blockade of, 37
history, 12–14
military power, 15
oil exports, 15–16
revolts against, 110
surrender, 108, *109*, 110
Islamic religion, 38, 39
Israel, 63, 64, 65

J
Jordan, 19

K
Khafji, Saudi Arabia, 72–74
Kurds, 15, 42, 110, 112
Kuwait, 5
aftermath of war, 112, *113*
history, 12–14
invasion of, 16–20
liberation, 85, 103–104, *105*
ruling family, 16
Kuwait City,
invasion of, 18–19
liberation, 103–104, *105*

L
Lebanon

M
Marines, U.S., 32, 36, 49, 51, 58, 66, 72, 73, 74, 75, 76, 78, 79, 82, 100, 103, 104
Missouri, *U.S.S.*, 36
multinational forces, 34, *35*, 36, 37, 59, 89, 104, 112
Muslims, 38, 110

N
National Guard, U.S., 114
Noriega, Manuel, 26
nuclear weapons, 42, 58, 61

O
oil, 17, 21, 47, 66, 67, 112
prices, 15–16
Operation Desert Shield, 22–24, 26, 27, 39
build–up of, 30–34
Operation Desert Storm, 114
air assault, 5–11, 55–57, 67–71
land assault, 74–79, 80–88, 89–98,
Organization of Petroleum Exporting Countries (OPEC), 15, 16

P
Palestine Liberation Organization (PLO), 7, 10, 38, 39
Panama, 26
Patriot missiles, 64, *65*, 66
Powell, Colin L., *25*, 26
leadership, 24, 28, 29, 47, 51, 61, 106
prisoners of war (POWs), 68–69, 87, 102, *103*

Q
quotas, oil production, 16

R
Reagan, Ronald, 26,
Republican Guards, Iraqi, 18, 20, 23, 90, 92–98, 108–109
Riyadh, Saudi Arabia, 28, 51
Rumaila oil field, 16

S
Sabah, Sheik Jabir al-Ahmad al-Jabir, 18
Sabah family, 16, 18
Saddam. *See* Hussein, Saddam.

Saratoga, *U.S.S.*, 31, 69
Saudi Arabia, 38, 39, 49, 64, 67, 74, 80
  Kuwait invasion and, 20, 21, 22, 28, 30, 32, 33
Schwarzkopf, H. Norman, 21, *27*, 28–29, 114
  leadership, 24, 26, 39, 51, 58, 61, 71, 106, 107, 108
Scud missiles, 59, 63, 64, 66
Shaw, Bernard, 5–11
Shepard, Gary, 5
Stalin, Joseph, 14

U

United Nations
  coalition forces, *See* multinational forces.
  Security Council resolutions, 21, 36–37, 52, 53
United States
  Arab nations and, 21, 28
  Kuwait invasion and, 16, 20–23
  Kuwait liberation and, 103–107
  popular support for war, 47–49
  preparations for war by, 21–22, 30–34, 36, 42,

W

Wisconsin, U.S.S., *7*, 31, 36
women, 39–40